A Vicarage Christmas

A Vicarage Christmas

The Holley Sisters of Thornthwaite

KATE HEWITT

TULE
PUBLISHING

Chapter One

NO ONE WAS waiting for her at the train station. Anna Holley knew she shouldn't feel disappointed; she hadn't said what train she'd be able to get from Manchester, only that it would be in the early evening. And the vicarage was a five-minute walk from the station, so it wasn't as if she needed a lift.

Still, she felt it, the self-pitying flicker of disappointment that was so annoying because it was silly. With a sigh, she hitched her backpack higher on her shoulder and started down the platform. An icy wind funnelling through the fells cut straight through her parka and scarf, stinging her cheeks and making her eyes water. *Welcome to Cumbria.* At least it wasn't raining.

Four days before Christmas, and in the starless darkness of an early evening, the village of Thornthwaite was nothing more than shadowy buildings huddled against the darker humps of the fells that cut a jagged line out of the horizon. Anna hadn't been back to Cumbria for three years, and she was amazed at how she'd forgotten how the fells made her feel, the way they rose up and surrounded her. Trapped, that was how she felt. The only way out of Thornthwaite was a single-track road that was often clogged with sheep. One had to drive on it for six painstaking, winding miles before they hit the A66, and then it was another twenty minutes to Keswick, and they were still pretty much in the middle of nowhere.

Still, it was beautiful, if you liked hills and isolation. No one else had got off at Thornthwaite—surprise, surprise—and so Anna walked down the platform alone, turning left over the little stone bridge that spanned St John's Beck, little more than an ambitious trickle as it wound its way through the village. She then started walking towards St Andrew's Church, the squat, square Norman tower lit up with Christmas lights at this time of year.

For a second, as she paused at the top of the lane that led to the church and the vicarage beyond, homesickness swamped her—a longing not just for the place, but also a time, when life had seemed simple and easy, and happiness was a foregone conclusion instead of something that always seemed to slip out of her grasp. Feeling that way seemed like a very long time ago now, not that anyone else in her family would share her sentiment. As far as Anna could see, everyone else was busy bustling around, seeming very happy indeed.

Taking a deep breath, she squared her shoulders and started up the lane. The stained glass windows of the church were lit from within and, as she walked by, the strains of a choir-led Christmas carol drifted out. It took Anna a moment to recognize it—"In the Bleak Midwinter". Yes, that summed her mood up quite well. Not that the weather was much nicer back in Manchester, but at least in Manchester there were lights and people and noise, and it was so wonderfully easy to be anonymous.

Here, in a village of two thousand, when your father had been the vicar of the only church for over twenty years, it was a little less so.

The vicarage loomed up ahead of her, an imposing square house with gabled windows on both storeys, the top decorated with sandstone crenulations. It had been built two hundred years ago, had eight bedrooms and eleven fireplaces, and it was freezing in both summer and winter. It was the only home Anna had known besides the boxy flat she shared with Helen, a woman she hardly ever saw or spoke to, and, looking it at now, she felt a rush of emotions she couldn't begin to untangle—hope and fear, love and dread.

She stood by the wide, worn steps leading up to the front door with its shiny black paint and ornate gold knob and knocker and wondered what she was waiting for. A welcoming committee? The courage to step into the happy chaos that had always been her home, while she drifted around its edges?

A shiver went through her as the wind continued to blow. She'd forgotten her gloves and her hands were icy, numb at the tip. Taking another deep breath, Anna marched up the steps and opened the door.

The Victorian-tiled porch looked as it always did, vast and lovably shabby, with a clutter of shoes in a basket by the door, another, bigger clutter of mud-spattered wellies on the other side, as well as an old church pew piled with post and church bulletins, plus the latest packet of parish magazines, wrapped in twine. Everything looked achingly familiar, as if she'd only been gone for a few days instead of years.

Anna opened the glass-fronted door and stepped into the downstairs hallway. Doors led off to her father's study, the living room and dining room and downstairs loo, and a wide, shallow staircase led up to the landing with its towering bookshelf filled with tattered paperbacks. How many times had she and her sisters bumped down the stairs on a pillow or blanket, squealing with both laughter and terror? How many times had Jamie—

But she wouldn't think about Jamie right now.

"Hello?" Anna called. She could hear Radio Four from the kitchen in the back of the house and Christmas music from the living room. She closed the door behind her to cut off the draught. "Hello?"

"Hello?" Her mother's musical voice came from the kitchen. "Eileen?" she called, referring to one of the church wardens who always seemed to be stopping for a cup of tea and a natter. "Has the service finished?" Her mother came around the corner, followed by their ancient, grey-muzzled lab, Charlie, and then down the hallway towards Anna, and then she stopped short. Charlie trotted forward, wagging his tail, and nosed Anna's knees.

"Anna." Within seconds Anna was enveloped in a floury hug. She put her arms around her mother, breathing in the scent of cinnamon and cloves. "I've just been making yet another batch of mince pies. We're having the choir over for mulled wine and mince pies after the Service of Lessons and Carols." Her mother stepped back to scrutinize her, eyebrows drawn together. "You look pale—"

"I'm cold," Anna said lightly. "It's freezing out there. And in here."

"Come in the kitchen. You know it's always warm in there. Esther and Rachel are coming over in a few minutes, for the choir party. We're going to decorate the tree tomorrow night, when everyone's here, even the new curate. He couldn't come until December—something to do with the new bishop. I can't keep track of it all." Nor could Anna, but before she could offer a reply, not that she would, her mother continued, "Rachel's got out all the decorations. We were looking at the ones you all made in nursery—pine cones and glitter galore. I was covered in gold dust as soon as I opened the box."

Anna had followed her mother back to the kitchen which was as cosy as she'd promised, the rumbling, red Aga emitting a wonderful warmth. Charlie flopped in front of it as Ruth Holley bustled around, spooning homemade mince into pastry cases, occasionally glancing at the Aga or the clock. "They should be coming over here in twenty minutes or so and I'm covered in flour… Anna, darling, can you stir the mulled wine? I'm afraid it's going to burn."

Anna went over to the Aga, stepping over Charlie's inert form, and stirred the vat of mulled wine simmering on its hot plate. It smelled deliciously Christmassy, of orange and spices and rich, red wine.

"So, how are you?" Ruth asked as she put a star-shaped piece of pastry over each mince pie, her fingers flying. "I feel as if I haven't talked to you in properly in months. You're always so busy."

"Work," Anna offered, half-heartedly. She wasn't *that* busy, but she wasn't very good about calling home.

"Do you know, even after four years, I'm not exactly sure what it is you do? Legal librarian." Ruth shook her head, marvelling. "I'd never even heard of such a thing until you got the job. Do you know Edith Mitchell researched it and wrote it up for the parish magazine? Everyone wanted to know what it is you're doing. We're all so proud of you."

"Thanks," Anna murmured. She leaned over the big pot of mulled wine and breathed in its comforting scents. She could do with a glass or two.

"I've kept the magazine for you. I'm not sure where…"

"It's fine." Anna straightened.

The kitchen looked as lovably messy as it always had, with the colourful jumble of mismatched pottery visible in the pantry, whose door had been taken off to be sanded down some twenty-odd years ago and never been put back on. The chairs around the big, rectangular table didn't match either; when one broke, her parents had bought another from a charity shop, or someone gave them a cast-off, and so now six entirely mismatched chairs, some tall-backed, some spindle-legged, gathered around the table of old, weathered oak.

Ruth opened the Aga and banged in two pristine trays of star-topped mince pies. Her mother was messy and always flying about, doing a dozen things at once, but she was an astonishingly good cook.

"So." Ruth stood up, brushing a wisp of grey hair out of her eyes and planting her hands on her hips as she gave her third daughter a good, long look. "You haven't told me how you are yet."

"I'm fine," Anna began, and before she could say more, not that she had anything planned, her mother was off again.

"I gave your bedroom a quick tidy. Daddy laid a fire but I think some birds must have nested in the chimney because it smoked dreadfully, so make sure you have a hot water bottle to take to bed with you."

"Okay." Anna had a sudden, piercing memory of the five of them lined up in the kitchen while her mother handed them each a fleece-covered hot water bottle. Everyone had a different colour; hers had been purple.

"Why don't you take a moment to freshen up? Trains

always make me feel so dirty. The choir will be arriving soon, and I know everyone is desperate to see you—"

"Oh, Mum." Anna's heart flip-flopped at the thought of being put on inspection practically the moment she arrived. "I'm really rather tired…"

"Oh, but, Anna, we've told everyone you're coming and you haven't been back in *years.*" Her mother's face crumpled a bit, and Anna bit her lip.

She knew she'd hurt her parents by staying away. Weekends in Manchester weren't the same. Her parents always made the effort to visit for a weekend every few months, and her sisters had come down a couple of times as well. Anna was the one who tried to avoid going home. In a way, she was surprised her mother noticed.

"I know you're busy," Ruth continued hurriedly. "I'm not saying you aren't, darling. It's just everyone really would like to see you."

Would they? Anna wondered. Would they really?

Ruth gave her another quick hug and then turned her around to aim her towards the door. "Go have a moment to relax. Shall I make you a cup of tea?"

The kitchen was still a disaster zone, and her mother had guests coming in about ten minutes. Yet she would gladly make Anna a cup of tea and bring it upstairs on a saucer with a homemade piece of shortbread if Anna said yes.

"I'm fine, Mum," she said. "I'll have a glass of wine when everyone comes."

Ruth brightened. "Lovely. I'll pour yours first."

Anna grabbed her bag from the hall and headed upstairs. The house smelled of the fresh evergreen that was looped around the banister, as it had been every Christmas that Anna could remember, tied to the burnished wood with little velvet bows.

Her bedroom was the small one over the kitchen; when she'd been about seven, she, Esther, and Rachel had all drawn straws to see who got the biggest bedroom at the front of the house, opposite their parents. Esther had, and Rachel had taken the second biggest by the stairs, and Anna had gone to this bedroom, a comfortable little square, warmed by the Aga below, its sashed windows overlooking the back courtyard with the old oil tank and the clothesline.

Anna didn't mind the lack of view; she'd always liked her room. She'd preferred it to the far grander bedrooms with their gabled windows and ornate fireplace surrounds. This room was warm and cosy and small and a little bit forgotten, tucked away by the corridor to the bathroom. Kind of like her.

It felt strange to step into it now; the air smelled of coal smoke, from her father's aborted fire, as well as her mother's lavender cleaning polish. The duvet cover was new, a blue plaid that was pretty enough but not the one from Anna's childhood, which had been grey and purple stripes. All her things were gone save for a few Famous Five books from her childhood, and a dusty blue ribbon for winning the high jump at her school's field day when she was thirteen that still hung from the mirror.

Anna put down her bag and then went to the bathroom with its ancient and enormous claw footed tub and pipes that squeaked and moaned when she turned the hot water tap; the water didn't heat up for a good five minutes. *Ah, home.*

She'd just come out of the bathroom, having washed her hands and face, when she heard an explosion of chatter downstairs, and a half-hearted bark from Charlie, who clearly wanted to get in on the action. Male laughter, and then the thunder of feet up the stairs.

"Anna!" Rachel catapulted herself towards Anna, hugging her tightly and making her stagger. "It's so good to see you."

Esther stood behind her, hands on her hips, smiling in a stern sort of way. "It's only been three years, after all."

"I saw you in August," Anna protested as Rachel gave her one final squeeze and then stepped back.

"But you haven't been back to Thornthwaite in three years," Esther remarked, typically. She'd probably been tracking everyone's movements on a spreadsheet.

"Well, I'm here now," Anna said as lightly as she could. She was battling a weird mix of dread and deep happiness, the two emotions so closely twined it was hard to separate one from the other. But this was always how she'd felt about home. About family.

"Come downstairs," Rachel said, tugging on her hand. "There's someone I want you to meet."

"Anna already knows him, Rachel," Esther said, rolling her eyes.

"Knows who?" Anna said with a flare of alarm.

She was *not* good about meeting new people. She wasn't even good at meeting people she already knew. Chitchat was her absolute nemesis.

"You'll see, you'll see," Rachel said, her feet practically dancing as she tugged Anna along. "It's all happened so fast… and I haven't talked to you in ages."

"True." Anna knew Esther and Rachel saw each other all the time, since they both lived in Thornthwaite. She was the odd one out, and always had been. Their younger sister Miriam was such a free spirit, as well as the baby of the family, and so even though she was in Thornthwaite even less than Anna, she had a place. A role. Neither of which Anna had ever felt she'd had… but that was probably her fault. "Who am I meeting, exactly?" she asked as she followed Rachel down the stairs, feeling apprehensive.

She'd really been hoping to hide in her bedroom while the choir came in, but perhaps she could still do that. She'd meet whoever it was Rachel wanted to meet, and then hightail it upstairs before the party got started. She was no good at parties.

"Rachel's latest," Esther said, following them down the stairs, and Rachel made a sound of protest.

"You make it sound like I've had a string of guys, and you know that's not true."

Esther didn't reply and Anna's steps slowed as she saw who was standing at the bottom of the stairs. Dan Wells. She took in the slow smile meant for Rachel, the warm hazel eyes, and her stomach plunged like a lift headed straight for the basement.

"Anna, you know Dan, of course," Rachel said, her voice ringing with the pride of a new girlfriend. "And, Dan, you know Anna…"

"We've met once or twice."

Anna forced a smile. She'd never been friends with Dan, although he'd been three years ahead of her in school, in Rachel's year, and of course she'd known him as the local vet. He'd given Charlie all his jabs and he'd also put down their beloved cat, Felix, when he'd been suffering and in pain a few years ago. He'd been Thornthwaite's only vet, having taken over the practice from his father, since he'd qualified five years ago. And before that…

Before that he'd been her secret and overwhelming teen-aged crush. But thankfully no one knew that but Anna herself.

Chapter Two

"I T'S GOOD TO see you, Anna." Dan transferred his warm, engaging smile to her as he stretched out a hand for her to shake. "It's been awhile."

"Yes." Anna shook his hand as quickly as possible, since her palm was clammy. Her heart was starting to hammer, and she had the awful feeling of marbles in her mouth that made speaking nearly impossible. She hated how this always happened to her. Hated it, and yet was helpless.

Everyone seemed to be waiting for her to say something, but she had no idea what. She opened her mouth to try, and nothing came out.

Fortunately, or not so fortunately, there was a commotion in the front hall as the members of the choir started to come in, pumped up and boisterous after the service of Nine Lessons and Carols.

"Anna!" Diane Tomlinson, a senior member of the choir who used to babysit the Holley girls when they were small, caught sight of Anna and bustled in, enveloping her in a tight hug before she could take a breath. "It's so lovely to see you, my angel. It's been so long."

Anna nodded, letting out a sigh of relief when Diane released her. But the other choir members were swarming in, exclaiming over her, over Rachel and Dan, over everything. Anna managed to just smile and nod—the noise and commotion prohibited actual conversation, thank goodness.

Esther was giving her a strange, piercing look, and Anna avoided her gaze. How she'd managed to disguise her social anxiety as mere shyness for twenty-two years was testament to how chaotic her family life was. It was easy to get lost in the noisy mix, and so often no one noticed she wasn't speaking at all.

Ruth came in from the kitchen having tidied her hair and changed her floury jumper, and was bearing a heavy-laden tray of mince pies.

"There's mulled wine in the kitchen… help yourselves. Anna, do you want to dole it out?"

Anna nodded, grateful for that semi-reprieve. The kitchen was quiet, Charlie having retreated to his place by the Aga after an introductory sniff of everyone, and Anna managed to dole out cups of mulled wine with little more than a smile and a murmured hello. That she could manage, especially when it wasn't a crowd of people all surrounding her and listening to her, *expecting* things.

"So what do you think to Rachel and Dan?" Esther asked when the initial stream of guests needing drinks had trickled off, and they were alone in the kitchen. Esther had folded her arms and was leaning against the kitchen counter, giving Anna one of her knowing, speculative looks. Esther always saw too much, and yet at the same nothing at all.

Anna took a deep breath and let it out slowly, forming each word in her mind before she said it. "They're dating, I gather?"

"Yes, they have been for about three months."

"Rachel never told me."

Esther shrugged. "I think she wanted to tell you in person."

"Hmm." It was easier to talk to Esther in the kitchen than out in the crowd, and the marbles-in-the-mouth feeling thankfully had dissipated. But Anna was still left with a leaden feeling about Dan and Rachel. She'd had a crush on Dan since she was about eleven. He'd always been so gentle in school, sporty and successful without being one of those callous jocks. He'd taken the time to hold a door, say hello, listen. And there had been a couple of times when he'd been especially kind to her, when the mean girls of year eight had ganged up on her, and she'd hidden behind the Eton Fives courts, not wanting anyone to see her cry. Dan had.

"Is it serious?" Anna asked, stirring the wine, and Esther shrugged.

"Seems to be."

Anna glanced at Esther, who seemed a little pricklier and more brusque than usual. "How are you and Will?" Esther had married local sheep farmer Will Fenton five years ago.

She worked for The Farmers Trust, a national charity that supported farmers in environmental practices. It meant she was often on the road, driving up hill and down in her mud-splatted Land Rover, visiting taciturn farmers in far-flung places.

Esther raised her eyebrows, seeming surprised by Anna's question. "Me and Will? We're fine. Why wouldn't we be?" If there was a slightly surly note of challenge in her big sister's voice, Anna decided to ignore it.

Esther had always intimidated Anna a bit; she was so self-assured and certain about everything, and she'd been incredibly driven in school, always at the top, whether it was lessons, sport, music. Esther was the kind of girl who was picked for everything and seemed unsurprised to be so, about as far as Anna was, hiding behind her books and trying not to be noticed. Sometimes Anna thought Esther was a little impatient, or even fed up with, her shyness. All through their childhood, Anna had hung back while Esther had stormed ahead, bolshy and brave.

"I don't know," she told Esther, backtracking quickly. "I just asked."

"Well, we're fine," Esther said, and it made Anna wonder if they really were.

"Now someone whispered in my ear that my little Anna was here."

Her heart lurched as her father came into the room, his weathered face wreathed in smiles, his arms opened wide.

"Hi, Dad." Anna let herself be enveloped in a big hug, breathing in the familiar, beloved scent of pipe tobacco, his not-so-secret vice, and bay rum aftershave.

Tears stung her eyes, surprising her. She'd seen him just a few months ago but it was different at home. Everything felt different at home, which was part of the reason she'd avoided returning to Thornthwaite for so long.

"You all right, Anna Banana?" he asked, using her childhood nickname. He drew back from their hug, squinting ta her. "You look like you need some fattening up. I prescribe a cup of mulled wine and at least three mince pies."

"Three?" Anna said with a little laugh.

"I intend to have at least four. You know they're my favourite."

"Yes, I know." Just about every baked item her mother made was her father's favourite.

"How's the big city, anyway?" he asked as he helped himself to the mulled wine and two minced pies cooling on top of the Aga. He popped the first one into his mouth in one bite.

"Big. Cityish." It was an in-joke between them, from a shared love of *Fawlty Tours*, to add "ish" to just about any word to describe something. "How's Thornthwaite?"

"Oh, you know. Villageish."

They grinned at each other and Anna felt some of the tightness in her chest ease. Maybe coming home wouldn't be as hard as she feared after all.

"Now you can't all hide in the kitchen," Ruth chided, coming in with an empty platter. "Roger, you need to circulate."

"I am circulating," her father said, and popped the second mince pie into his mouth. "With my daughters."

Ruth rolled her eyes good-naturedly. "You know what I mean."

"I'll circulate," Esther said, and pushed off from the counter. Ruth watched her with a slightly worried frown.

"Is everything all right with Esther?" Anna asked, and her mother turned to her with a sigh.

"I think so. Not that she tells me much about anything. You know Esther."

Yes, she knew. Esther liked to boss people around and organize everything, but she was notoriously closed-lipped about her own life.

"Come on, Banana," Roger said, loping an arm around her shoulders. "Let's go make chitchat." The understanding smile made Anna realize he knew this was hard for her. He just had no idea how hard.

"Yes, go on, you two." Ruth shooed them out, smiling, and so Anna had no choice but to walk with her dad out of the kitchen and towards the dining room, where everyone had gathered.

The high-ceilinged room was garlanded with fresh evergreen, a cheerful blaze roaring away in the fireplace. Anna knew almost all the choir members by name, but whether she knew them, *they* knew *her*. Even after so many years as a vicar's kid, it was disconcerting to be addressed in an entirely familiar fashion by someone she only vaguely recognized. Even the choir members who had joined since she'd left Thornthwaite for uni ten years ago seemed to know who she was, as well as all the details of her life, or at least the ones she'd shared with her parents.

After just ten minutes of nodding and smiling and offering the occasional word, Anna was starting to feel dizzy. And then the marbles-in-the-mouth feeling came back and, even worse, Diana Tomlinson asked her in a ringing voice when she was going to bring a boyfriend home, and it just happened to be during one of those silences that naturally fell upon a crowd every so often.

The only sound was the crackling of the logs in the grate and the ticking of the grandfather clock as everyone waited for Anna's answer.

"Umm... ummm..." Her face started to flame and someone in the crowd gave a kindly laugh.

"Cat got your tongue, Anna? Maybe there is someone."

Anna stared at them all in helpless misery, knowing she wouldn't be able to manage a word.

"I'm sure my Anna is beating off the boys with a stick," her father said in his genial way.

Anna saw the frowning concern in his eyes and felt the awful welter of shame. She was such a *disappointment,* even if her parents would never say as much.

"Hugh," her father called, turning to a red-faced man who had scoffed two glasses of wine already. "Where did you say you were going for New Year's? Edinburgh?"

The conversation duly started up again, like someone flicking a lever, and Anna took a step back from the crowd, feigning a fascination with her cup of mulled wine. People left her alone, which was what always happened after one of her spectacular conversation fails.

Everyone stepped around her for a while, as if she was an unexploded land mine they all had to avoid, or maybe just something messy and unpleasant they'd rather not step in. And then they eventually forgot about it, or pretended to, and tried again. Rinse and repeat. It was a cycle Anna had been desperate to break out of, and things had been a bit better in Manchester, without all the expectation of being known, without the burden of shared memory and grief. Unfortunately, she was still essentially the same.

She edged through the door, wondering if she could escape upstairs without anyone noticing, or at least caring. People would just feel even sorrier for her, but that was okay. She was used to it. Another step, and she was in the doorway. Then she was in the hall, and she was turning for the stairs when she saw Rachel and Dan sharing a kiss under the mistletoe that had been helpfully placed above the front door.

"Anna!" Rachel let out a little laugh and stepped back from Dan, smiling and blushing.

Anna averted her eyes; she didn't want to see Rachel and Dan in some kind of clinch. Her crush on Dan had been of the schoolgirl variety, hopeless and yearning, but it had been intense. And it wasn't as if she had a ton of experience with the opposite sex as it was.

"You're not leaving the party already?" Rachel exclaimed. Her second oldest sister always seemed surprised by Anna's proclivity to stand on the sidelines, mainly because Rachel was such an out-and-out extrovert herself.

"I'm... tired," Anna hedged, cringing inside, as she noted Dan's narrowed look of concern.

"Why don't you hang out with us instead?" Rachel suggested. "We were going to sneak upstairs and watch Netflix anyway." One of the vicarage's bedrooms had been turned into a private sitting room for family, since the downstairs rooms were so often used for meetings and guests.

Anna envisioned the three of them squashed on the sofa, watching a rom com, and tried to school her expression into something that wasn't a wince of horror. "Actually... I think... I'll take a walk." The words came out in awkward, staccato bursts. "Thanks anyway," she added, grateful that she was starting to sound more normal. Another deep, even breath.

"A walk?" Rachel looked incredulous. "It's freezing out."

"It's been... so long... since I've been back. I'll be fine." And not trusting herself to say anything more, Anna hurried towards the front hallway, grabbed her coat and scarf and a spare pair of mittens from the drawer that was always full of mismatched ones. She stuffed her feet into mud-splattered wellies and then yanked open the door, shutting it as quietly as she could behind her before heading out into the night.

If anything, it had become colder in the hour since she'd arrived back in Thornthwaite, colder and darker. She set off down the lane, the church now silent and empty, the stained glass windows sightless and dark. Anna shivered. She had no idea where she was going. Thornthwaite at eight o'clock at night did not exactly offer a host of amusement.

The village had two pubs—The Bell Inn and The Queen's Sorrow, which had something to do with Henry VIII's last wife Katherine Parr, whose residence had been in nearby Kendal. The Bell tended to be a bit rougher, if Thornthwaite could be considered to have a rough element, and The Queen's Sorrow was the go-to pub for ladies' nights out, pub quizzes, and even the VSA's termly meetings.

Out of instinct, Anna headed for The Queen's Sorrow, needing somewhere warm to go because wandering through the village on a freezing winter's night was not an option. But then right in the middle of the little stone bridge crossing St John's Beck, she stopped, because she was sure to know someone at The Queen's Sorrow and the last thing she wanted right now was to have to make chitchat with a well-meaning parishioner. She craved anonymity, but how did she get that in a village of two thousand where she'd spent the first eighteen years of her life and her dad was the vicar?

She went to The Bell.

The Bell was on the corner of Thornthwaite's two main streets, the unoriginally named High Street and the far more interestingly titled Finkle Street, which Anna knew from the town's well-versed historian came from the Danish word for corner. And Finkle and High did form a sharp, steep corner on which The Bell beckoned with its bright red door, raucous laughter heard from within.

Taking a deep breath, Anna opened the door and stepped inside. Thankfully, no one took any notice of her at all, which was both a surprise and a blessing. The pub was far too busy, and people seemed far too drunk, to care about a slight young woman swathed in a parka coming through the door.

Anna squeezed her way between a group of twenty-something men in football jerseys singing a laddish song and a couple of fortyish women wearing makeup and tight tops who looked like they were on the prowl. This was a whole side of Thornthwaite she'd never even known existed. Until this moment, she'd never stepped so much as a toenail in The Bell before.

Amazingly, she found a bar stool, right down at the end. A man was sitting next to her, elbows braced on the scarred oak of the bar as he sipped thoughtfully from a pint, his gaze distant and distracted. On the other side a couple of women were having an intense discussion, their dyed heads bent close together.

Anna slipped onto the stool and surveyed the rows of bottles behind the bar, amazed that she'd dared to get this far. But then speaking to strangers had never been a real problem; crowds of unfamiliar people didn't scare her too much. No, it was the people she knew who rendered her petrified and speechless.

After a few minutes of being overlooked by the bartender, a beefy man in a tight white t-shirt, the man next to her lifted his shaggy head and called out in a surprisingly educated sounding voice,

"Pardon me, but I believe this young woman would like some service."

Anna blushed and squirmed as the bartender swung his narrowed gaze towards her. "Yeah? What you want, love?"

"Um…" Her mind went blank. Totally, stupidly blank.

The mulled wine seethed in her stomach, but she could hardly ask for that.

"White wine? Red wine? Cider?" The man next to her suggested helpfully in a murmur. "Or perhaps something soft?"

"Cider," Anna said definitively. She hadn't drunk cider since her student days, but so what? She felt a bit reckless all of a sudden.

The bartender looked bored. "What kind of cider?"

Mind blank. Again. "Ummm…"

"Can I recommend the elderflower?" the man next to her said. He had a funny, lopsided, and strangely endearing smile. "Refreshing and not too sweet."

"Thank you—"

"And"—he added, his smile deepening to reveal a dimple in one lean cheek—"would it be too forward to ask if I can buy it for you?"

Chapter Three

ANNA STARED AT the stranger in shock, because she couldn't remember the last time someone had offered to buy her a drink. And he didn't look like the kind of guy who was buying a drink expecting something; he just seemed nice. Still, she wasn't sure how to respond.

"I won't, if you'd rather I didn't," he said as his smile became even more lopsided. "Just tell me to mind my own business."

"I don't care who pays for it," the bartender informed them curtly, "but what is it you want, love?"

"I'll have the elderflower cider," Anna said. She offered the man an uncertain smile. "And yes, you can pay for it, if you're of a mind to."

"I am."

The bartender disappeared to fetch her drink, and the man held out his hand. "Simon."

"Anna."

They shook hands awkwardly and then Anna settled more comfortably on her stool. Tucked in the back of a bar she'd never been in before, with a friendly stranger, she felt more at ease in Thornthwaite than she had in a long time. No one's assessing eyes were on her, no one was looking expectant or hopeful or, worse yet, disappointed. No one was looking at her at all, except for Simon, who was smiling, having no preconceived notions about her at all. Hopefully.

"So are you visiting here, Anna?" Simon asked, and she shook her head.

"No, I live here. Or I should say lived here. I'm in Manchester now. I'm just back, visiting my family."

"You've got me there, then. I'm—what do they say? An offcomer?"

"Yes." Anna looked at him appraisingly. Slightly shaggy, sandy brown hair, a cleft chin and dimples, and hazel eyes that looked both friendly and warm. He was like the human equivalent of a Golden Retriever, the kind of person one instinctively trusted and liked. And yet he had none of the pathetic eagerness of a dog desperate for affection... no, Simon the Offcomer seemed perfectly happy to sip his pint of bitter and let the silence stretch on.

The bartender returned with her cider and as Anna lifted the glass, Simon raised his. "Cheers."

"Cheers," she said, and took a sip.

"Well?" Simon asked when she'd put the glass down. "Your verdict?"

"Refreshing and not too sweet. Thanks for the recommendation."

"Anytime."

They sipped in silence for a few minutes while Anna wondered whether she wanted to keep the conversation going. Would her parents have noticed her absence? Would her mother be worried? The next ten days back in Thornthwaite stretched on endlessly. Her mother would be trying to make everything as Christmassy and wonderful as possible, her father would be his affable, cheerful self… and Anna would be quietly suffering, straining to seem like each moment spent back here wasn't costing her.

Why had she agreed to come for so long? Her mother had practically begged her, telling her that Dad had the whole week off after Christmas, and they had some news to share. What news, Anna couldn't even imagine. Getting another dog? Buying a timeshare in Majorca?

"So what brings you to The Bell?" Simon asked. So, they were going to keep talking.

"Well…" Anna hesitated, wondering how much to share. Simon was a stranger, but a nice one, and somehow she didn't think he'd judge her. "I had to get away," she confessed in a split-second decision to unburden herself and tell the truth.

"Family holidays?" Simon surmised with a grimace. "They're not always easy."

"No." Anna ran her finger along the rim of her glass, pensive. "But mine aren't what you'd think. No drunken fights or snippy comments… nothing like that."

Simon settled himself more on his stool. "What, then?"

"It's just so hard," Anna said in a rushed whisper. She stared at her glass, not quite able to look at him. "Everything seems so perfect on the outside—like a Sainsbury's ad or something."

"But underneath?" Simon prompted after a pause, his voice gentle.

"Underneath, it's all wrong," Anna admitted. She felt a rush of guilt at saying that much. "Not wrong, exactly, but… it's as if we've papered over this huge, gaping crack and no one is ever going to acknowledge it."

"I think plenty of families do that. It's normal, even if it's not right. And eventually you have to find a way to fill the crack or fall in it."

"Yes, exactly." Anna turned to look at him, surprised and gratified by his perception. "But the trouble is… what if you've already fallen in?" Until she'd said the words she hadn't realized just how much she meant them.

Saying it out loud was like acknowledged the gaping wound in her chest that she'd pretended to ignore, staggering on and on. Acknowledging it meant it was still there, it was still serious and maybe even life-threatening, but at least she could dress it. She could see a doctor, get help. Couldn't she?

"Is that what's happened to you?" Simon asked. His gaze was steady and kind, without even the hint of judgment or, worse, pity.

Anna let out a long breath. "Yes, I think so."

"And have you tried to get out?"

"I don't think I can." Anna let out a shaky laugh and took a sip of her drink. "I think this metaphor might have gone on a bit too long."

"You're undoubtedly right," Simon agreed with an affable nod. "Most metaphors do."

"So why are you in The Bell just four nights before Christmas?" She didn't know if she regretted telling Simon as much as she had; it had felt weirdly freeing, confessing that much.

Maybe she should seek some kind of therapy. She'd always been afraid to, but now she wondered... although chatting for five minutes to a stranger in a bar was a far cry from lying on a sofa, spilling her secrets.

"I just moved here and I don't know anyone," Simon answered with a shrug. "I thought I'd try my local."

Anna eyed his beat-up cords and button-down shirt. "I think you'll find more congenial company at The Queen's Sorrow."

Simon chuckled. "You don't think I fit in here?"

"Well, you haven't looked at the TV screen once to check the football score, and it's Man U playing West Ham."

"Ah, caught out." He shook his head in mock regret. "I'm more of a cricket man, myself."

"Why am I not surprised?"

"Are you stereotyping me?"

"No..." Anna protested, and then laughed. "Well, maybe a little bit. Let me guess. You went to Oxbridge?"

"Only for a postgraduate degree."

"You went to boarding school."

"Day school but, yes, it was private. All boys. Somewhat awful."

Were they flirting? It felt a bit like it, in a very non-threatening and mild way, which was probably all she could handle. "What brought you to Thornthwaite? Do you work at Sellafield?"

Most people worked at the nuclear power station about half an hour away.

"No, different field altogether. What about you? You said you live in Manchester?"

Was he avoiding answering her questions? "Yes, I'm a legal librarian."

"A legal librarian? I didn't know such a thing existed."

"That's what most people say. I keep the research and information current for a law firm. It's a rather solitary job, just me and my computer in a cubbyhole, more or less."

"You like it?"

"Yes." She liked the familiarity of it, the safety, and the consistency. But did it make her heart beat harder, in a good way? No. Not much did.

"So, Anna, about this crack you've fallen into," Simon said after a moment, and she let out a bit of a groan.

"Not the metaphor again."

"Sometimes it's a bit easier to use metaphors."

"Yes, I suppose."

"But, if we're not using metaphors, what exactly do you mean? Do you get along with your family?" He looked so genuinely concerned for her, his hazel eyes crinkled at the corners, that Anna found herself blurting out the truth.

"They think I do. They think everything is pretty much fine. I feel like I'm the only one who realizes—" She stopped abruptly, feeling she'd said too much. Simon was going to think she was a complete nutter, and maybe she was.

"Who realizes…"

Anna drained her half-pint of cider. "If I'm going to tell you anything more," she said, "I need another drink."

"Then let me be forward again and buy you one." He raised an arm to flag down the bartender. "Same again?"

"Why not?"

⋙⋘

SIMON WATCHED AS Anna stiffened her shoulders and stared ahead resolutely. He didn't want to get her drunk, but he could tell when someone needed to talk. All part of his training, not that he'd tell Anna that right now. He didn't know quite what she meant about falling into a crack, but she was hurting and he wanted to help her. That was the whole reason he'd changed careers and moved up to the back of beyond from London. To help people. And to feel needed.

The bartender came back with Anna's cider, and she took it with murmured thanks. She was a lovely woman, with porcelain skin, her cheeks flushed a delicate pink, and a cloud of dark hair. Her eyes were dark too, a deep navy, although it was hard to tell in the dim lighting of the pub. Perhaps they were grey. She was swathed in a parka and wellies, but she seemed slender, as if a breath of wind might blow her away and, in Cumbria, that could very well happen.

"So, you were telling me," he prompted after she'd taken a sip. "You're the only who realizes…"

She shot him a look that wasn't suspicious, not exactly. "Are you a therapist or something?"

"No." Not exactly.

He smiled, wondering if he was pushing too hard, but he was curious about her. There was something so contained and intense about her sadness, as if she kept it so tightly inside that the pressure of it was slowly killing her. He hoped that wasn't the case.

He also hoped, in some small way, he could help. Because he knew what it was like to watch someone suffer, and feel totally helpless. He never wanted to feel that way again, ever. Which meant he might have gone into the wrong career. Simon acknowledged this point wryly as he took a sip from his own half-pint and waited for Anna to say something.

"I'm the only one who realizes that something is wrong. That everything is wrong." She closed her eyes briefly, shaking her head. "It's all built on a fake foundation."

"And no one else knows that?"

"If they do, they're not acknowledging it." She gave him a rueful look, but Simon still saw the sadness in her eyes, like storm clouds on the horizon. "I know I'm speaking in vague riddles. The truth is, I have what everyone thinks is the perfect family. And they are amazing, in their own way. I've never doubted that my parents love me, or love each other, or my sisters, either. Everyone's brilliant." She sighed, her shoulders slumping. "Except me."

"Why aren't you brilliant?" Simon asked gently.

With her shoulders slumped, she looked as if she was carrying the weight of the world on them.

"Everyone thinks I'm just shy," Anna confessed in a rush. "But I'm not. It's much more than that. That's why I don't come home, because I can't take all the scrutiny, all the well-meaning questions, all the expectations." She let out a shuddery sigh. "It's too hard. And I start to—" She gave him an uncertain look. "I should stop now, shouldn't I?"

"When it's just getting interesting?" Simon answered. "You don't have to tell me anything, Anna. But it sounds as if you need someone to talk to."

Anna was silent for a moment. "It's easier, talking to a stranger," she admitted. "Someone I'll never see again."

"You might see me again," Simon warned her. "I do live in Thornthwaite now."

"Yes, but I don't."

"True."

"The truth is," Anna said in a low voice, her gaze on the scarred and sticky top of the bar, "I'm not just shy. I have... I have social anxiety. When I get in crowds of people, people I know who are asking me questions, I... I have a sort of panic attack, and I start to... I start to stammer." She let out a whoosh of breath. "And no one knows."

Simon was silent for a moment, considering this. "Then you've done a bloody good job of hiding it."

"Yes, well." She gave him an embarrassed smile, blinking rapidly. "Everyone just thinks I'm terribly awkward."

"And you'd rather they think that then know you have a condition?"

"Yes, I suppose I would. A condition." She shuddered. "That sounds so awful."

"Plenty of people—"

"Oh, I know, I know. I've looked up the statistics online. I've even done exercises to try to stop it, but I know it's psychological. I tell myself it's just mind over matter, but it isn't. At least, it doesn't feel that way to me."

"Did you always have it, even when you were young? Because I imagine it would be more difficult to hide as a child."

Anna was silent for a long time, and Simon waited, not wanting to press. Her hair had swung forward to hide her face, and he had the entirely inappropriate impulse to tuck it behind her ear, skim his fingers along her cheek. He was *not* going to chat up a vulnerable young woman in a pub. This wasn't about that. It couldn't be.

"It started when I was eight," Anna answered quietly, her eyes downcast. "When my brother Jamie died."

"I'm sorry," Simon said, meaning it utterly. He knew how hard grief was, a long, lonely slog, with no end point in sight. Eventually one just got used to the slogging, but sometimes they realized how tired and never-ending it was, and they wondered whether it was worth going on.

"We don't talk about it," Anna continued, her gaze still firmly fixed on the bar. "We talk about him. We're not totally dysfunctional."

"Well, you know what they say. A dysfunctional family is one with people in it."

"Right." She gave him the glimmer of a smile, although her expression was still haunted. "But we've always talked about him. We remember his birthday and we toast him at Christmas. We talk about him, his goofiness, some of the expressions he used that were so funny—" She broke off, swallowing hard, and Simon resisted the urge to touch her hand, to offer her that comfort.

"How old was he when he died?"

"Ten, two years older than me. It's how he died that we don't talk about it. The day it happened. What I—" She stopped again and brushed at her eyes. "Sorry, you must think I'm a complete basket case."

"No, I really don't." No more than he or anyone else

36

was, anyway.

Everyone struggled. Everyone suffered. And just about everyone tried to slap a smile on it.

"Well." Anna took a deep breath and let it out slowly. "Let's talk about something else." She reached for her barely-touched cider and drained the glass.

"All right. How long are you back in Thornthwaite for?"

"Ten days. My father has some announcement he and Mum want to make. They're probably going to do the coast-to-coast walk or something." She sighed wearily. "Sorry if I sound cynical."

"You don't. Pragmatic, maybe."

"Where are you from?"

"Outside London. Nameless, boring suburb."

"You're a long way from home, then."

"Yes, but I wanted to go somewhere I could be more known. And I've always loved the Lake District. Fell walking and all that. I'm probably going to have to get a dog."

"Dogs do seem a prerequisite here," Anna agreed.

She looked up from her drink, her lips slightly parted, her eyes a bit glassy. She was, Simon suspected, more than a little bit drunk, and on a pint of cider.

"You know why I came out here tonight?"

"Why?"

"To get away from my sister and her boyfriend. They surprised me, when I first got home. It was hard enough just being there and then Rachel announced she was dating

Dan." Anna shook her head, her lips pursed, while a frisson of recognition went through Simon. Rachel… Dan… "I had a crush on him when I was in school," Anna confessed with a hard, little laugh. "Stupid, schoolgirl thing, but it felt pretty massive at the time. He saw me crying once… I was bullied, in school," she said by way of explanation. "For the whole socially awkward thing. Mum and Dad never knew. But I suppose the crush took on this importance it never really had because the truth is, I've never had a proper boyfriend. The truth is, I've barely been kissed." She looked up at him with wide, sad eyes. "Isn't that pathetic? I'm twenty-eight years old."

"Not pathetic," Simon said carefully. He had a feeling Anna was going to regret telling him all this in the morning, especially now he had a feeling he knew who she was. "You're just waiting for the right person."

"I am," she agreed, and hiccupped. "I'm just not sure he exists."

"And I'm sure he's out there. But it is getting a bit late. May I walk you home?"

"What? Oh, I'm fine." She shook her head. "I might have another cider…"

"I don't think that's a good idea," Simon said as gently as he could.

Anna's widened. "Oh no, do you think I'm drunk? *Am* I drunk?"

"I think maybe a little," Simon answered with a smile.

"But you tell me."

She paused, wrinkling her nose. "I don't know. I only had two half-pints of cider, but I didn't eat anything today except for a sandwich on the train."

"I think," Simon said, "the best thing for me to do is walk you home."

"That's not necessary—"

"I'm a gentleman. Humour me."

With a huff, Anna slid off the stool and pushed her arms into the parka she'd slipped off at some point in the evening. Simon dropped a pound coin on the table for a tip and then put one hand lightly on the small of her back to steer her through the press of the drunken crowd.

"The Bell's not that bad, actually," she said once they were outside in the crisp, clear night.

Simon breathed in the cold air, marvelling at the beauty all around him. A sliver of moon illuminated the jagged peaks of the fells that surrounded the village on every side. In the distance, a sheep bleated, the only sound save for the rustling of the wind.

"Let's get you home," Simon said, and started towards the bridge that led to the church and the vicarage beyond.

Anna stopped right there on the pavement. "How do you know where I live?"

"I don't," Simon answered honestly, because he wasn't sure and now was definitely not the time to explain who he was. "Why don't you tell me?"

Anna started walking, brushing past him and starting towards the bridge. "This way," she called back. "But you don't have to come. I'm fine."

Simon followed her, all the way to the lane that led to the church. Then Anna turned to him, looking soberer than she had in the pub. Perhaps the cold air had helped.

"I can take it from here. Thank you for listening, Simon." She gave him a crooked smile. "We probably won't see each other again."

"I was glad to meet you, Anna." And he decided not to tell her that they most certainly would meet again, in just a few hours. They could both cross that bridge when they came to it.

With a little wave, Anna turned and started down the lane. Simon watched until she was swallowed up in darkness, and then he waited until he heard the distant creak and click of the front door of the vicarage opening and closing. Then he turned and started back to home.

Chapter Four

ANNA WOKE UP to sunlight streaming through the window and a foul taste in her mouth. She blinked fuzzily, aware that someone was tapping on her bedroom door.

"Anna? Darling? I've brought you a cup of tea."

Anna scooted up in bed, her head pounding with the effort of moving. Goodness, but she was a lightweight. Two glasses of cider and she'd practically passed out. She was still wearing most of her clothes from last night; all she'd managed to do before falling asleep was wriggle out of her jeans.

Ruth peeked around the door, holding a tray with a mug of tea and two pieces of toasts slathered with marmalade and butter, her favourite.

Anna blinked back the sting of tears. "Thanks, Mum. You're amazing."

"I didn't even realize you'd gone out last night," Ruth said, and Anna could tell her mum was trying to keep both the worry and censure from her voice. "I was so busy with all the choir… they can be a noisy lot, can't they?"

"Yes, they can." Anna took the mug from her mother with murmured thanks, curling her fingers gratefully around its warmth.

"Were you meeting someone?" Ruth asked as she picked up Anna's crumpled jeans from the floor and folded them. Her mother always tidied when she was feeling nervous or unsettled.

"Yes, a friend." She supposed she could sort of call Simon that, and she didn't want her mother to know she'd stormed out of here without a plan, or that she was sad enough to drink in The Bell by herself.

"From school?" Ruth said hopefully, and Anna just shrugged.

She didn't want to lie outright, and she'd lost touch with most of her school friends. Her best friend from secondary, Josie, had moved away after uni and now lived in Portsmouth, working at the university there. Although they kept in touch via social media and email, Anna hadn't seen her in years.

"Well," Ruth said when she realized Anna wasn't going to answer. "We've got a big day planned. Esther and Rachel are coming over with Will and Dan, and the new curate is already downstairs, meeting with Dad. I thought we'd invite him too, to decorate the tree. He doesn't know a soul here yet, poor chap."

Anna nodded, steeling herself for a day of chitchat and pleasantries with her family and this unnamed curate. Her father had had a procession of curates through the years, and, depending on Anna's age, they'd either been big brothers, unrequited crushes, or gangly youngsters. Absently she wondered what this one would be like.

"I thought I might take Charlie for a walk," she said. Preferably along the fells, where she wouldn't run into a single well-meaning soul.

"Oh, but you'll be here for lunch, won't you? And the tree?"

Anna knew she couldn't avoid these kinds of interactions forever. It wasn't fair to her parents or her sisters. She'd come home because her parents wanted her there, to decorate the tree and go to the Christingle service and hang up the stockings on Christmas Eve. Even if Anna found all those things both bittersweet and hard.

"Yes, I'll be here for the tree," she promised her mother. "When is it, exactly?"

"I thought after lunch. I'm doing a roast."

Her mother's roasts were wonderful. That, at least, was something Anna could look forward to without reservation.

"Can I help?" Anna asked, taking a sip of sweet, milky tea.

"You're always brilliant at the Yorkshire puddings," Ruth said with a smile. "You have the magic touch."

Anna smiled back, remembering how as a teenager the Yorkshire puds had been her provenance. Almost every Sunday growing up, they'd had people from church over for dinner, and Ruth had assigned each of the children a job to do, giving them more responsibility as they'd grown older. Anna had started by laying forks when her head barely cleared the table, and gradually moved up to the Yorkshires. Jamie's last job, she remembered with a pang, had been laying fires in the dining room and sitting room fireplaces. Right before he'd died he'd been given the great responsibility of lighting them.

"Sure, I'll do the Yorkshires," she said now, trying to hold on to her smile.

Her mother smiled back, looking pleased, and Anna wondered if Ruth was as tormented by the past as she was. She knew her mother was still sad about Jamie; she saw it sometimes, in the faraway look she'd get in her eyes, the slight slump in her shoulders. But did she torture herself the way Anna did, remembering those poignant little details, each like a stab to the heart? Did her sisters? Her dad? No one ever *said* anything. No one ever talked about the accident, and whose fault it had been.

"I'll leave you to get ready, then," Ruth said as she laid Anna's folded jeans on the end of the bed. "I'll see you downstairs."

Alone in her bedroom again, Anna sipped her tea and nibbled the toast, even though her stomach rebelled against both. She leaned her head against the pillow and closed her eyes, fragmentary memories of last night drifting through her mind, puzzles pieces that slowly slotted together to form a

A VICARAGE CHRISTMAS

whole, unappealing picture.

She hadn't done anything really stupid, at least. She was glad of that. She remembered saying goodbye to Simon and walking down the lane towards the vicarage. She also remembered blurting some things out in the pub... about her family and feeling lost, and how she stammered. Why on earth had she told a stranger *that?* Even her family didn't know or, if they did, they didn't acknowledge it. Anna didn't know which prospect hurt more.

With a sigh, she put aside her tea and toast and rose from the bed. From downstairs, she could hear the happy clatter of a busy home—pots and pan, Charlie's lethargic bark, as if he couldn't be bothered, and her father's low voice and someone's answering reply, presumably the new curate.

Soon Rachel and Esther would be coming over, and Dan and Will, and the house would feel full and happy... to everyone but Anna. Was she the only one who felt adrift, lost amidst the happy chaos? Was she the only one who kept remembering, who kept wishing things were different?

Anna closed her eyes briefly, trying to banish the painful questions she didn't want to ask, much less answer. It was so hard coming back here after so many years away. So, hard when every corner of the house, every tradition or joke or throwaway remark, seemed to hold a memory.

She took a shower and dressed quickly in jeans and a fleece, standard Cumbrian wear. Outside the sun was, rather amazingly, shining, and, from her window, she saw the churchyard with its ancient, lopsided headstones, every blade of the tussocky grass glittering with frost.

There was no real reason to stay upstairs any longer, and so, after a moment's hesitation, Anna made her way downstairs. Although it was barely nine o'clock in the morning, lovely roasty smells were emanating from the kitchen. Anna made her way to the back of the house and the comforting warmth of the room that had always felt like the heart of the home.

To her surprise, her mother wasn't bustling around, making three dishes at once; rather she was sitting at the kitchen table, a cup of tea forgotten by her elbow, her head in her hands.

"Mum..." Anna called softly, her heart lurching.

Ruth looked up, startled, and then quickly smiling. "Anna. You look much better. Do you want anything else? A scrambled egg, or some bacon?"

"I think you've got your hands full here, Mum." Anna took a step closer; Charlie's tail thumped against the ground at her approach and she leaned down to fondle his ears. "I'm fine. Can I help? What's the roast?"

"Pork. I just put it in so it should be ready by one, when we're eating. But if you want to help, why don't you ask your father if he'd like a cup of tea? The curate's just arrived and I haven't had time to get him a cuppa."

Even though she'd got Anna one. Anna suspected her mother might be doing a spot of not-so-subtle matchmaking, and once again Anna wondered about the curate, picturing someone kindly but just as or even more socially awkward than she was.

"Sure, Mum," she said, and went to knock on her father's study door.

It was mostly closed but not shut; there had always been a rule in the vicarage that if her father's study door was completely closed, no one was even to knock. If it was mostly closed, then knocking was allowed. Roger said this was to keep private pastoral situations confidential, but Anna suspected he just wanted some guaranteed peace and quiet.

Now she knocked lightly and was rewarded by her father's affable, "Come in, come in!"

Anna pushed the door open, blinking in the wintry sunlight streaming through the gabled windows. Her father's old mahogany desk, passed down from his own father, was piled with papers and books and vacated at the moment. Roger and his most recent curate were sitting in the worn leather armchairs in front of the fireplace, feet stretched out to the flames.

"Anna, my dear," Roger said, and Anna smiled at him.

"Mum wanted to know if you'd like a cup of tea or coffee. The kettle has just boiled." She turned to the curate sitting in the chair opposite, and then the smile froze on her face.

It was Simon.

>>>><<<<

SIMON SAW THE stricken look flash across Anna's face and wished he could have spared her this moment. Perhaps he should have told her who he was last night, at least after he'd begun to guess who she was, but, by that time, she'd been two if not three sheets to the wind, and Simon hadn't felt he could.

"Anna, meet Simon Truesdell, my newest curate, just come up from London."

Anna's horrified gaze was fixed on him as she opened her mouth. No words came out. Simon remembered what she'd said about stammering and he hurried to fill in the silence.

"Nice to meet you, Anna. A cup of tea would be lovely. Shall I come and help?" At least then he'd be able to explain.

She nodded wordlessly, and Roger looked on, benevolent and oblivious. Anna turned on her heel and Simon followed her out into the draughty entrance hall which was, thankfully, empty.

"Anna—"

She shook her head. "D-d-d-don't."

"I'm sorry," Simon persisted in a low voice. "Perhaps I should have said something last night, but there didn't seem to be a good opportunity—"

"D-d-d-did you know who I was?" she asked without looking at him. "The whole time?"

"No, I didn't know at all. I started to wonder, perhaps, at

the end, when you mentioned Rachel and Dan, because your father had said something about them, but I promise you, I didn't chat you up knowing you were."

"Is that what you were doing?" She turned to him with a scathing look. "Chatting me up?"

"No." Horrified, Simon shook his head with force. "I meant, I *wasn't* doing that. I didn't know who you were until the end of the evening, and then it was only a guess." At that moment, Simon doubted the wisdom of just about everything he'd done—coming to Thornthwaite, going into ministry, certainly talking to Anna last night and buying her a drink.

Anna just shook her head and walked swiftly to the kitchen. Feeling entirely out of his depth, Simon followed her.

"Oh, Simon, you didn't have to help," Ruth exclaimed as Anna switched on the kettle and grabbed the tin of teabags.

"I don't mind," Simon said rather miserably.

Anna refused to look at him, and it hurt him more than he'd expected. Naturally, he didn't want to get off on the wrong foot with his boss' daughter, but it was more than that. He didn't want to get off on the wrong foot with Anna because he liked her. He wanted to count her as a friend, and, right now, he suspected she saw him as an arch enemy. And all because he'd let her say too much last night. Should he have stopped her? Could he have?

"Here you are," Ruth said cheerfully, and put a couple of

shortbread biscuits on a plate to take in with their tea. "You will stay for lunch and decorating the tree, won't you, Simon?"

"I…" He glanced at Anna, who was purposefully not looking at him. To refuse for Anna's sake would seem rude to Ruth. And, really, although she might want him to, he couldn't avoid Anna forever. He didn't want to. "Yes, thank you. That will be lovely."

Without a word Anna took the mugs of tea back towards the study. With a last smile for Ruth, Simon followed her.

"Anna." He tried once more, as they were at the study door. "Please…"

She just shook her head, her lips pressed together. Simon realized she wasn't giving him the silent treatment; she was just surviving, and his heart ached for her.

"I'm sorry," he whispered, and she thrust the mugs at him without another word.

TORTURE. THAT WAS what this was. Pure, sheer torture. Anna got through the next few hours by simply blanking her mind. She helped her mum with the dinner, laying the table and whisking up the batter for the Yorkshire puddings, managing to keep up somewhat of a conversation with Ruth so her mother didn't suspect anything.

Every once in a while, a stray memory would slip in, and

inwardly she would cringe and squirm. She'd told him about her crush on Dan, and that she'd never had a proper boyfriend and barely been kissed. Mortification didn't begin to cover it. What on earth had possessed her to spill all her tightly-held secrets to a stranger who now, unfortunately, *wasn't* a stranger?

Just before lunch, Rachel and Dan came in on a gust of cold air, followed by Will and Esther. Esther seemed even more tightly wound than usual, but Will was his usual taciturn self, although Anna noticed he seemed to take special care of Esther, fetching her a drink, resting his hand on her waist when they were the anti-PDA couple if there ever was one. What was going on there?

She didn't have too much time to think about it because then her father and Simon were emerging from the study, with introductions all around, and then they were all retiring to the sitting room with thimblefuls of sherry. Anna tried to stay in the kitchen helping her mum with dinner preparation, but she shooed Anna out and so she had no choice but to join the others, sitting tensely on the edge of her seat and enduring. She couldn't look at Simon, couldn't bear to see the pity written on his face.

The conversation swirled around her as it so often did, and thankfully Anna didn't have to make much contribution at all, which was par for the course. She could feel Simon looking at her, imagined him trying to assess her family's dynamics based on what she'd said last night. *It's as if we've papered over this huge, gaping crack and no one is ever going to acknowledge it.* She felt miserably disloyal to her family for saying such a thing, even if it felt true. And she hated Simon knowing it, along with everything else.

Her mother finally called them all into dinner, and then she assigned seats to everyone as she always did, and of course she put Anna next to Simon. Her mother was definitely doing a spot of matchmaking, and it couldn't have come at a worse time.

The trouble was, Anna reflected as she passed the potatoes and poured the gravy, in different circumstances, back in the safety of the city perhaps, she might have fancied Simon. He was kind and interesting and she liked his warm eyes, the way they creased at the corners. She even liked his rather shaggy brown hair, and underneath his polo jumper and cords he looked to have a rangy, muscular body, no doubt from all that fell walking he did. But she couldn't like him now, not when he knew so much about her. Not when the first emotion he'd ever experienced with her was awful, wretched pity. And certainly not when he was her father's curate.

Chapter Five

LUNCH FELT INTERMINABLE. The conversation swirled around her, mostly about village news and Christmas plans, as Anna picked at her food.

Simon turned to her once with a smile. "The Yorkshire puddings are delicious. Ruth said you made them?"

He was throwing her a bone, and she tossed it right back at him. "Yes." End of conversation. If she had the emotional energy, she'd feel sorry for Simon; he so obviously wanted to make things right between them. But she felt far too raw for that, and eventually he turned to Rachel, on his other side, and chatted about her job as the year three teacher at Thornthwaite Primary. And somehow that bothered her too, even though Anna knew she was being unreasonable.

Simon probably thought she was having a childish stop, she reflected miserably as her mother served the pudding, hot apple crumble with custard. Even she could see how seemingly petty she was being, and yet she couldn't help it because having someone know everything she'd held hidden forever was the equivalent of peeling back her skin, nerve endings pulsing and raw. How else could she act in such a situation? She was just trying to protect herself as best as she could.

"What's got you in such a funk?" Esther asked when they were in the kitchen scraping plates. Anna tossed a juicy sliver of pork fat into Charlie's bowl.

"A funk? What do you mean?"

"You're more silent and sulky than usual, and that's saying something."

Esther spoke in her usual, matter-of-fact way, not unkindly, but, stupidly, it still stung. Sulky? "I'm just tired."

"And why did you storm out of the party last night?"

"I didn't storm out." Fled, was more like it. "I wasn't up for facing the entire church choir the minute I got home. Surely you can understand that, Esther. You don't like the choir dos at the best of times." In part because her sister had quit the choir in secondary, and Nigel, the choir director, had never forgiven her.

"Whatever." Esther shook her head. "Something's going on with you, Anna."

They moved into the sitting room for tea, coffee, and her mother's delicious homemade petit fours while they decorated the tree. Roger put on some Christmas carols and when a few snowflakes drifted lazily down outside, it felt particularly festive, with the York Minster Choir belting out "God Rest Ye Merry Gentlemen" from the CD player, and a fire crackling merrily in the grate.

"A white Christmas," Dan said jokingly, and Anna watched as he slipped his arm around Rachel's waist and kissed her cheek.

Watched also as her sister gave him a distracted smile and slipped out of his embrace to fetch another ornament, this one a Styrofoam ball enthusiastically sprayed with gold glitter that flaked off the second one touched it. Something seemed slightly amiss there, or was Anna just paranoid because she felt so out of sorts herself?

"Look at this one," Simon said, and picked up a sterling silver snowflake with a red velvet ribbon from the box. "Is it an heirloom?"

"It belonged to my mother," Ruth said with a small smile. "She had the most amazing collection of ornaments, all very elegant. My sister and I split them between us when she died."

Simon held it out with a smile. "Then perhaps you should do the honours."

"Oh, I don't mind," Ruth answered with a laugh. Her gaze darted hopefully to Anna. "Why don't you hang it on the tree, darling? You haven't hung any yet, have you?"

"No, she hasn't," Esther chimed in.

Her sister was obviously keeping her eye on her.

Wordlessly Anna rose and took the ornament from Simon. Their fingers brushed as she took the ribbon and she felt the most inconvenient frisson of attraction. Even more alarmingly, she thought Simon felt it too, judging by the way his hand jerked a little as she took the bauble. That was the last thing she needed in the present circumstances. Anna turned away and went to hang the snowflake on the tree, conscious of everyone's eyes on her.

"Well done," Roger said in a too-jolly tone that made Anna feel as if she were six. Why couldn't any of this be *easy?*

Anna gave her a father a quick smile and sat back down on the sofa, wanting only to be ignored. She caught Simon's eye and before she could look away she saw the expression on his face—pity mixed with regret. Everything she'd told him reeled through her mind and she closed her eyes. This was interminable. A few seconds ticked by before someone broke the silence, saying something about the tree, and Anna snapped open her eyes.

"I think Charlie needs a walk," she announced, and Ruth looked up startled.

"Oh, but we've just started—"

They hadn't just started; they'd been in the sitting room for nearly an hour. The York Minster Choir carols was on its second playing, and the tree was mostly decorated. The only thing left were a few bargain baubles and the star at the top, a cardboard cut-out covered in kitchen foil that had graced their tree since before Anna could remember.

"I think he needs some air," Anna said firmly. "I'll be back soon." She left before anyone could make another protest, calling for Charlie and then hurrying to the entrance hall where she yanked on wellies and her parka, praying no one would follow her and make a fuss. She needed to be alone, to absorb and accept Simon's presence in her family's life, as well as the knowledge he possessed.

Looping the lead around Charlie's neck, she zipped up her parka and started outside. Although it was only a little past three, the sky was already darkening to lavender, the snowflakes that had been drifting down from inside the comfort of the cosy sitting room now stinging her face.

Charlie loped along as Anna strode down the church lane and then turned left, out of the village, towards the footpath that led up through the fells. She'd never been much of a hiker; she hadn't been sporty as a child and city living suited her that way, but now Anna battled valiantly up the ever-steepening path, past prickly gorse bushes and winter-flowering heather until she emerged on a relatively level path that followed the shape of the fell and overlooked the village now quite far below.

It had been a long time since Anna had been up on the fells, and she breathed in the clean, icy air and felt the tightly held parts of herself loosen a little bit. The sky was wide and endless up here, with vivid streaks of lavender darkening to grey, and the first stars beginning to twinkle on the horizon.

She took off Charlie's lead and let him run about and sniff as she walked down the path towards a look-out over Thornthwaite with an old, weathered bench. Anna sank onto it gratefully and closed her eyes, conscious that it was getting dark and even colder, and that being up on the fells in such weather, even such a low elevation as this, was not entirely wise. Still she didn't want to move. The thought of returning to the vicarage with everyone's well-meaning worry felt suffocating. She couldn't bear it, not yet.

"Do you mind if I join you?"

Anna let out a little shriek of surprise and opened her eyes. Simon stood in front of her, hands dug into the pockets of his North Face jacket, smiling sheepishly.

"I do, actually," she replied, but she moved over so he could sit down. "Why did you follow me?"

"I wanted to talk to you."

"You could have let me know you were behind me."

"You were walking too fast. I could barely keep up as it was."

Anna sighed. "And I suppose everyone saw you leave the vicarage right after me? What are they all going to think?"

"I'm not that daft, thank you very much," Simon said lightly. "Your mother asked me to go after you. She thought you were upset."

Anna rolled her eyes. "She's not exactly subtle, is she?"

"What do you mean?"

"Nothing." The last thing she wanted to was explain about her mother's attempt at matchmaking. If Simon didn't see it, she certainly wasn't going to point it out.

"I came after you really to talk to you. About last night. To apologize—"

"For what exactly?" Her words came out thankfully sharp

and clear.

He'd caught her on the back foot earlier, and she'd been reduced to an anxious, stammering wreck but she felt better prepared now. *Somewhat* better prepared.

"For putting you in a difficult position. That wasn't what I meant do at all."

"Why didn't you say you were the new curate?" Anna asked. "I asked you if you worked at Sellafield, and you just said you were in a different field. But it was as if you were hiding it."

"I suppose I was," Simon answered after a pause. "Not for some nefarious reason, but because I'm not here officially yet, not till Sunday when I'm licensed. The bishop told me I needed to keep a low profile."

"So you went to the pub."

"Is that a crime?" he asked lightly. "I had a bit of cabin fever. I moved up here a week ago and the only person I'd met was your father. He's lovely, but I was going a bit stir crazy, a bit lonely."

Anna stared out at the stunning view, now mostly shrouded in darkness. Lights appeared in the darkness, cosy cottages and narrow terraced houses. She could see the star lit up on the church tower, like the beacon it had been some two thousand years.

"Why did you get me to say all that stuff?" she asked in a low voice. "I'm not blaming you for the fact that I spilled my guts, but you certainly encouraged it. You kept asking me questions, kept prompting me…"

"I wanted to help." Simon sounded wretched. "Honestly, Anna, that was it. You seemed like you needed to talk, and I thought I could be that person. It wasn't until you mentioned Dan and Rachel that I realized we'd see each other again. Not," he added quickly, "that I regret that. I know you're angry with me right now, but I hope we can be friends."

"Friends?" Anna asked in a voice choked with disbelief.

"Why not? Is it so terrible, that I know a few things about you?"

"Is it so terrible?" Anna repeated slowly. She turned to look at him and, in the gathering dusk, she could barely make out his features. That made it easier to say what she knew she needed to. "Simon, I know it must seem like I'm being petty or childish, to hold last night against you. I know it wasn't your fault that I said everything I did, especially after that second cider. But…" She took a deep breath, willing herself to go on even though her heart was starting to beat hard and she was beginning to get that choking, marbles-in-the-mouth feeling. "You have t-t-t-to understand," she said painfully, her voice low, "how completely t-t-t-terrifying it is for me to have someone know all my s-s-s-secrets." She took another deep breath, willing herself to calm. "All the things I've kept to myself, I've hidden on purpose, and it's cost me a lot to do that, and now s-s-s-someone who knows my family, will s-s-s-see them every day…" She shook her head, unable to go on. Her throat had closed up and her eyes stung with tears.

"Anna." Simon put his gloved hand on top of hers. She could feel the warmth of his palm even through the fleece. "I'm so sorry for making you feel so vulnerable. That was not my intention, I promise you. And I hope you can come to understand and believe that I would never, ever use anything you said against you. I'd never think worse of you, either. If anything, I think you're brave."

"Brave?" she repeated disbelievingly with a big, revealing sniff. "How?"

"Because you've had a lot of sorrow and suffering to deal with it and you're still here," Simon said.

"That's not saying all that much."

"Actually," he said bleakly, "it is."

His tone gave her pause, and she wondered what made him say such a thing, and with such conviction.

"Tell me something about yourself," she said quietly. "Since I've told you so much."

Simon was silent for a long moment, making Anna wonder if he was going to say anything. It had grown so dark that she couldn't see his face at all.

"Well?" she asked shakily. "Isn't there anything—"

"There's plenty," Simon replied. "I'm just thinking what to say."

"Something embarrassing," Anna said. "Since I told you so many embarrassing things."

Simon lapsed into silence again, and Anna waited, wondering what he was going to say, if anything. "I was bullied in school," he said at last. "That's not exactly embarrassing, but it's something personal I don't tell everyone."

"Why were you bullied?" Simon didn't seem like the type of person to be bullied. He was so relaxed and confident, at ease in himself.

"It was in primary. I was a rather gawky lad—all skinny knees and elbows, and I had a bit of a know-it-all attitude as well. Not a good combination."

"So what happened?"

"A couple of blokey boys decided to make my life a misery. Every day in year five, they'd find me, corner me, and do something dreadful. Sometimes it was just a pinch or a slap. Other times it involved my head and a toilet."

"Oh, Simon." Anna stared at him, appalled. "But that's awful. Didn't you tell anyone?"

"I was too embarrassed. I didn't want anyone knowing I was getting the daylights kicked out of me on a regular basis. But I should have—it ended up making me so unhappy and anxious that I went off ill for weeks, and then my mum home educated me for year six, which was the longest, dullest year of my life, but it was still better than facing primary again."

"I'm sorry."

He shrugged. "It was awful at the time, but then I started secondary and found a good group of mates and it was fine. I recovered, but it still leaves a mark." He paused. "Doesn't it?"

"Yes." Anna scuffed her welly along the ground. "I wasn't bullied like that. I was just labelled weird and so I kept to myself. A Chinese girl came to the school in year ten, and no one liked her, either. So, we became best friends by default." Funny, she hadn't thought of Joanne Chang in years. She'd barely been able to speak English, and Anna hadn't had a word of Chinese, but they'd clung together out of necessity. After school, Joanne's family moved to South-ampton, and Anna never saw her again. They kept in touch for a little while, but it hadn't lasted. Sometimes Anna wondered if anything did.

"Then it seems we're not so different, at least in some respects." Simon shifted on the bench. "Now, it's getting really rather dark and I think your family is worried about you. It's not good to be on a fell after sunset, so I think we should head down."

"All right." Looking around, Anna realized just how dark it had become. A few stars glimmered in the sky, and the moon slid behind a bank of clouds. "You don't happen to have a torch, do you?"

"Just the one on my phone."

"I didn't even bring my phone." She felt a pang of fear. It was cold up there, and more experienced hikers than she had got lost and died on a fell in winter, never mind at night. What had she been thinking?

"Come on," Simon said gently, and reached for her hand. "It'll be okay."

And Anna, strangely enough, believed him. She let him draw her to his feet and then, with Charlie trotting by her side, she followed him down the narrow footpath that was lit only by the pin-prick beam of the torch on Simon's phone. The wind that funnelled through the fells was much colder than it had been a mere hour ago, when the sun had been starting to set. Every trace of warmth had vanished, leaving nothing but cold, bitter iciness.

By the time they reached the bend in the path as it went steeply down, the lazy snowflakes that had drifted by had turned into needling sleet. Anna looked down the steep, narrow path lost in darkness and felt another tremor of fear. She, who had grown up in the Lake District, had made a newbie offcomer's error, going out unprepared and at the wrong time.

Simon squeezed her hand. "Don't let go," he said seriously, and then started down. Anna clung to him, inching her way down the steep path, Charlie pressed close to her side. It felt as if they were walking forever, inch by treacherous inch, the friendly lights of the village never seeming to get any closer.

Her nails dug into his arm as her feet slipped on the path and she collided into him, sending them both stumbling. Anna let out a stifled shriek as she started to tumble, envisioning an endless fall down the hillside, but then Simon righted himself, drawing her close to his body.

All at once Anna was conscious, achingly so, of several things—the solid strength of Simon's chest, the protective shelter of his arms, and the immediate sense of total security that she felt, wrapped in his embrace, as her feet found solid ground.

He stroked her hair as he murmured, "Are you all right?"

Anna nodded, her heart still hammering in her throat. She didn't want to move. Simon didn't seem to want to either for he simply stood there, his arms around her, for another minute or two, until Charlie whined and Anna let out a shaky breath and started to draw away.

"We should go…"

"Yes." Simon stepped back carefully on the steep, rocky ground, and then, still holding her hand, he led her down towards the welcoming lights of Thornthwaite.

Chapter Six

WHEN ANNA CAME downstairs the next morning, the house was surprisingly empty save for Charlie, who was looking mournful, curled up by the front door. Anna scratched him behind his ears and tried to savour the quiet she hadn't had since she'd come back home.

Last night, after she and Simon had returned to the vicarage, her family had, predictably, made a complete fuss of them both, as if they'd been lost in a blizzard for two days instead of gone, as it turned out, for a little over an hour.

"Anna, we were so worried," Rachel had exclaimed, while Esther had watched with folded arms and narrowed eyes, and her mother had insisted they both have a tot of brandy 'for the shock'.

Anna tried to keep it low-key, insisting she'd just gone for a walk and forgotten how early it got dark this time of year, but no one seemed to be listening to her. It was like being caught in an undertow of noise and bustle; eventually she just gave up, drank her brandy, and let people cluck around her. At one point, she'd caught Simon's eye—she seemed to have a habit of doing that—and he'd given her a smile of amused complicity, so far from the pity she'd been afraid to see. She'd smiled back, and something inside her that had been tight and hard and heavy had inexplicably loosened and lightened.

Simon had left soon after, and Anna had retreated from the noisy hubbub of her family to her room upstairs, where she'd watched Netflix on her phone and tried not to feel guilty for causing such a stir.

Now she wandered around the downstairs, surprised to see that even her father's study was empty—she'd have expected him to be hard at work on a sermon or something. The kitchen was empty as well, although her mother had left a note on the table.

I'm delivering the parish newsletters and Dad's out with Simon. There are eggs and bacon in the warming oven, and the coffee in the pot should still be warm. Back soon. Love, Mum.

How her mother kept so many plates spinning all the time Anna had no idea. She made three hot meals a day, had a constant parade of guests through the vicarage, delivered the parish magazine, taught Sunday school and spoke at the Mother's Union meetings, as well as a thousand other things, while her family, Anna acknowledged with an uncomfortable prickle of guilt, more or less took her for granted. And Ruth never seemed to mind.

Anna took the bacon and eggs from the oven and poured herself a mug of coffee. She wished she could talk more honestly to her mother, and to her father and the rest of her family, for that matter. She loved them so very much. And yet there seemed to be this yawning chasm between her and them, and she had no idea how to bridge it. Her parents and sisters didn't even seem aware of it.

That gaping crack she'd gone and fallen in, just as she'd told Simon. Could finally coming back to Thornthwaite help her to clamber out? Or would she just fall in deeper still?

Anna was finishing the last of her eggs when the front door opened with a gust of cold wind, and she heard her sister's Rachel cheerful and breathless voice.

"Anybody home?" Before Anna could reply, Rachel came into the kitchen, her eyebrows raised as she caught sight of Anna. "You're on your own?"

"Mum's delivering magazines and Dad's out with the curate."

Rachel's eyebrows went higher. "You mean Simon?"

"Yes." Anna didn't even know why she'd called Simon "the curate", as if he were a stranger, but Rachel had obviously noted it.

"A moment of peace, then," Rachel said after a pause when Anna suspected she'd been debating whether to press her yet again about last night's abrupt departure. "I've just come by for the service bulletins for the carol service for school. It's in the church in an hour—are you going?"

"Going?" Anna hadn't been to one of the village school carol services since their younger sister Miriam had finished year six. "I didn't…"

"My year threes are singing 'Silent Night' on recorder." Rachel's mouth curved as Anna winced. "Surely you don't want to miss that?"

"Twenty eight-year-olds screeching away? Of course not."

"Bah humbug," Rachel said good-naturedly, but Anna had the uncomfortable sense her sister was a little hurt by her careless remark.

Rachel was fiercely proud and devoted to her year three class, and this was the first time since she had started teaching that Anna had been home for the end-of-term service.

"I suppose I could," Anna said, trying to inject a note of enthusiasm into her voice. "Get into the Christmas spirit."

"It does seem like you could use a dose of festive cheer." Rachel frowned. "Everything's all right, isn't it, Anna?"

The way she phrased the question was classic Holley family. Papering over all those cracks. Seeing what they wanted to see, hearing what they wanted to. Anna loved them all, but sometimes they filled her with despair.

"Yes, of course," she said. "Everything's fine. Why wouldn't it be?" She'd meant to speak lightly but it came out a little bit like a challenge, a question she wanted answering for real because she was so tired of pretending everything was absolutely fine. Perhaps that was why she'd ended up spilling her guts to Simon over a half-pint of elderflower cider.

"I don't know. Just making conversation. I'm glad you're doing so well." Rachel started the inevitable backtracking. "So, are you coming to the service? Because you should head over soon. A lot of eager parents are already there, warming the pews."

"Which is quite a feat." The church, with its soaring nave and antiquated portable heaters, was cold even in the height of summer, although "height of summer" in the Lake District could still mean snow.

"All right," Anna said as she rinsed her plate and mug and then put them in the dishwasher. "I'll come over."

Rachel left soon after with her arms full of service sheets, and Anna brushed her hair and teeth, giving her rather wan reflection a rueful look before she shrugged into her parka and headed outside.

The sky was low and grey with billowy clouds that promised snow but might not deliver, the air sharp and cold. Anna dug her hands into the pockets of her parka as she crunched across the gravel on the way to the church.

It had been a long time since she'd made this short walk, from house to church; she hadn't been back to Thornthwaite for a Sunday or special church service since uni, except for Esther's wedding five years ago. Roger had taken the service, wiping a tear from his eye as he'd pronounced Will and Esther man and wife.

A montage of memories flitted through her mind now—harried Sundays when her mother spit-washed them in the entrance hall of the vicarage before chivvying them over to the church, breathless and inevitably a little late. A few of the older members of the congregations had thinned their lips in disapproval at their tardiness, but most people had smiled tolerantly, glad simply to see young people filling the pews.

Anna recalled a round dozen of nativity plays, where she'd progressed from a sheep to an angel to a shepherd to a wise man. In year six, she'd been offered the role of Mary, as her sisters had been before her, but Anna had had to refuse. No way could she have stood up in front of everyone and said those lines. *Who am I, that an angel of the Lord should come to me?* She'd been a stagehand instead.

Now the head teacher of the primary, Sheila James, greeted her with a cheery if slightly distracted hello as Anna came in through the doors; a couple of year six boys were meant to be handing out service sheets but were making paper airplanes out of them instead.

Anna took one with murmured thanks and slipped into the last pew. She breathed in the familiar, musty scent of the church—dusty velvet mixed with candles and a hint of freshness from the flower displays adorning each ancient pillar. The church was full of proud parents and all the schoolchildren of Thornthwaite Primary, ranging from the angelically docile to the devilishly unruly. The poor little reception years looks tired and dazed; the year sixes were either bored or self-important as they did all the scripture readings.

Anna leaned back against the straight-backed pew and tried not to think about the service in this church that hovered on the edge of her memory, a constant, dark shadow. She'd been in here hundreds if not thousands of times but it was that bleak day that she remembered the most. The day of Jamie's funeral.

The casket had been so *small*. Her father, who had taken every baptism, wedding, and funeral—hatch, match, and dispatch, as he said—in Thornthwaite for ten years at that point, had not been able to take that service. A neighbouring vicar had done it, and Roger Holley had sat in the front pew with his family, his face drawn into stark lines of grief.

Anna flipped open the service sheet, determined not to remember. It looked like the service hadn't changed since she was a child—the pupils sang the same songs, gave the same readings. She supposed there was no point messing about with a good thing.

"Sorry, I'm not doing this on purpose, but do you mind if I sit here? Everywhere else is taken."

Anna looked up to see Simon smiling at her apologetically as he gestured to the empty stretch of pew next to her. The church was full; more parents had come in, and even the folding chairs placed at the end of many of the pews were occupied.

"No, of course not," Anna said, determined not to seem

petty. "Please." She scooted over a little more as Simon sat down.

He was wearing his usual cords, although these weren't so battered as the pair he'd had on at the pub, and a polo-neck jumper with a collared shirt underneath. His hair was still the same unruly mane, although he'd clearly attempted to tame it with a brush and some water. He gave her a quick, sideways smile, his eyes glinting warmly. Anna had a sudden, vivid recollection of the way he'd held her out on the fell, his hard, solid body pressed to hers. A shudder went through her at the memory that she quickly repressed. No point thinking of Simon that way, not now.

Thankfully, the service started, precluding any conversation, and Anna settled in to listen to a dutiful recitation of the second chapter of Luke. *In those days Caesar Augustus issued a decree…*

"They were all quite good, weren't they?" Simon said when, an hour later, the service had finished with a rousing rendition of "O Come All Ye Faithful". "Quite sweet, even the recorders."

Anna let out a little laugh. "I'm not sure my eardrums will ever be the same. I don't know how Rachel manages it in the classroom every day without earmuffs."

"I suppose she gets used to it." They left the pew together, navigating the press of eager schoolchildren who were now free for two weeks of Christmas holiday.

"How come you weren't up there with Dad?" Anna

asked. Her father had introduced the service and led the prayer at the end, as he did every year.

"Not till Sunday. That's when it's all official."

"Just two more days then." And Monday was Christmas Eve. "You'll be thrown right into it," Anna remarked. "All the service on Christmas Eve and Christmas."

"I don't mind. No other plans."

"What about family?"

"My parents live in Spain." Simon shrugged. "To be honest, they don't do really do Christmas, not properly."

"What did they think of you going into ministry?"

"They think I'm completely daft." Simon smiled, but Anna thought she saw the shadow of sadness in his eyes. "We never even went to church when I was growing up."

"Then how did you come to be a curate?"

"University. My best friend was keen and dragged me along to church. It felt right, and it made sense." He shrugged. "I never thought I'd go into ministry full-time, though, but here I am."

"And what were you before you trained to be a curate?" Anna asked, more and more curious about him. He looked to be about thirty, so he hadn't gone straight from uni to theological training like some of her father's previous curates.

"I studied history at uni then did my PGCE. I was a history teacher at a fairly rough school outside London for five years before going to theological college."

"That must have been hard."

"But very rewarding." He smiled. "I hope this will be even more so."

They'd reached the front doors of the church where Anna's father was greeting and shaking hands with the steady stream of parents and pupils. "Anna, Simon!" He smiled, looking pleased to see them both. "Was the service a stroll down memory lane for you, sweetheart?"

"Yes, a bit," Anna answered. "Funny how it hasn't changed at all."

"Oh, they always talk about changing it, but people are sentimental about these things." He appraised them both, his eyebrows raised. "What are your plans today?"

"I thought I might do a bit of Christmas shopping," Anna began at the same time Simon said, "I need to go into Keswick to do some Christmas shopping." They stopped and stared at each other, surprised and a little abashed.

Roger chuckled indulgently. "Sounds like a date to me," he said, and turned to the parents waiting behind them.

"We don't have to go together," Simon said once they were out of the church, the air damp and cold. "No matter what your father said."

Anna dug her hands deeper into her pockets and hunched against the cold. "Actually, I wouldn't mind," she said, surprising them both. "I can't drive so I'd have to take the train to Windermere or Carlisle, and it takes ages. If you don't mind giving me a lift…"

"I'd be happy to," Simon said. "Of course. More than

happy. I'm just glad you're not avoiding me."

"I'm not that childish," Anna answered, meaning to sound light but it came out a bit querulous. "I just had to get used to the idea that knowing all that about me, you're going to be close to my family."

"And you're used to it now?"

"No," she admitted frankly. "But I'm getting there."

Simon nodded in acceptance. "When do you want to go to Keswick?"

"Anytime. I just need to get my bag."

"Shall I pick you up in front of the vicarage in fifteen minutes or so?"

"Okay." As Anna walked back home, she realized she was looking forward to going to Keswick with Simon.

It would be good to get away from Thornthwaite for a bit and, yes, she was glad it was with Simon. Even though he knew too much about her, even if it made her feel weak and exposed and raw, she still liked him as a person and she wanted to get to know him better. The realization brought a tremor of trepidation as well as of excitement. This was whole new territory and while it wouldn't seem like much to some, or even most, it was a lot to her.

Her mother had just got home when Anna opened the door, Charlie rushing her as Ruth shrugged out of her coat. "Were you out at the service?" Ruth asked as they moved into the kitchen and she switched on the kettle, as she always did. "Was it lovely? I'm sorry I missed it this year, but I don't think I could bear hearing the same songs yet again." She gave Anna a ruefully apologetic look. "Is that awful?"

"Not at all. There are only so many kiddie carol services one can endure."

"I've always admired how your father keeps it fresh for himself. He always seems so genuinely pleased to be there."

"Yes." Roger had the gift of looking at life with enthusiasm, no matter what. Almost.

"I should have gone this year, though," Ruth said, sounding sad suddenly. "If I'd been stronger, perhaps…"

"What do you mean, Mum?" Anna looked at Ruth in growing alarm. "Stronger? For a carol service?"

"Oh, nothing." Ruth waved her away as the kettle clicked off. "I'm just being sentimental, because of the season." But Anna felt it was more than that, and she had no idea what.

"Is everything okay, Mum?" She realized how rarely she asked that question. Her parents always seemed so happy, so busy, bustling through their lives, and she tended to take them at face value… just as the rest of her family did to her.

"Fine, fine." Ruth concentrated on dunking teabags in mugs, and Anna had the feeling she was not meeting her eye on purpose. "Just a bit tired, perhaps. What are you up to today, darling?"

"I'm going to Keswick with Simon to do some Christmas shopping."

"Oh, lovely." Ruth looked up, her face flushed with

pleasure, and Anna sighed.

"Don't get any ideas, please, Mum."

"Ideas, what ideas?" Ruth said with too much innocence. "If you make it to Booth's, could you pick up some sherry? We're just about out and the wardens are coming over tomorrow evening. You know how Edith Appleton likes her tipple."

"All right."

A knock sounded on the front door, and Anna went to open it. Simon stood there, looking just as he had when she'd left him at church, but for some reason the sight of him caused a sunburst of pleasure in Anna's heart.

"Hey."

"Hey."

They smiled at each other for another moment and then Anna reached for her bag. "Onwards to Keswick."

Simon opened the passenger door of his beat-up Volvo, making it feel even more like a date. Except of course it wasn't, not even remotely. He was just giving her a lift. They'd probably split up as soon as they reached the car park. Anna settled back into her seat as Simon started down the church lane. No, this most certainly wasn't a date.

Chapter Seven

SIMON GLANCED SIDEWAYS at Anna sitting in the passenger seat, her expression pensive and peaceful. At least, he hoped it was. He couldn't always tell what Anna was thinking, but she seemed to have, for the most part anyway, got over her reluctance at being with him. And that was a good thing.

Yet in the short time he'd spent with her, Simon realized it wasn't enough. He didn't want to be tolerated. He didn't even want to be simply liked. And maybe that was unwise or even crazy, but he felt a connection with Anna Holley that he hadn't felt with another person in a long time. He felt an attraction too, and that part of him had been dead for so long he was amazed to feel it springing back to life. But it was, and it had been since Anna had first come into The Bell, looking flushed and pretty and sad all at once.

From the first moment he'd seen her, Simon had wanted to take away that sadness and that *was* unwise. He couldn't take away someone's sadness. He was no one's rescuer; that much he'd learned, and in the hardest way possible.

"I've been thinking," he announced, and Anna turned to him, her eyebrows raised.

They'd left Thornthwaite and were now driving down the single-track lane that led to the A66, steep-sided, snow-covered fells on either side of the narrow road. It was breathtakingly beautiful, and Simon hoped he never took it for granted. He didn't think he'd ever get tired of it, at least.

"You were thinking?" Anna prompted. "Are you going to tell me about what?"

"Yes, sorry. Just admiring the view. I was thinking about everything you told me." She grimaced and he hastened to add, "Not like that. Not the particulars. Just… the fact." Anna's mouth tightened and she didn't reply, just looked out the window as the rust-coloured fells streamed by. Simon wondered at the wisdom of bringing all this up again. Anna seemed to poised to put it behind her; why had he gone and ripped off the plaster of silence?

He knew why, of course. Because he couldn't leave things alone. Because he had a compulsion to make things better, to rectify and heal, and sometimes that was a good thing. Sometimes it wasn't. In any case, it never was enough.

"I was thinking about what you said last night, about how terrible or painful it was for someone to know all your secrets." Anna let out an audible breath and said nothing and resolutely Simon ploughed on. "But what if it's not terrible or painful? What if it can be a relief, Anna? Because the reason anyone keeps secrets is so people don't know about it, whatever it is, the worst or the weak or whatever. And the reason someone doesn't want anyone to know is because they're afraid what people will think when they find out. They're afraid of being judged or rejected or something else... but what if that doesn't happen? I know, Anna, and I'm still here. I'm enjoying spending time with you, and I'd... I'd like to get to know you better, even knowing what I do."

Anna was silent for a long moment. *"Even* knowing?" she repeated finally, her voice toneless, her face still turned towards the window.

"I didn't mean it like that."

"I know." She shook her head, biting her lip. "I just don't want you to think differently about me. To f-f-f-feel sorry for me."

"I don't."

"Are you sure?" She turned to him suddenly, her expression sharp and fierce. "Are you absolutely s-s-s-sure? Because I've seen the expression on your face, and sometimes it looks a lot like pity."

"I felt sorry for you yesterday," Simon said carefully, determined to be honest. "Because you were in a difficult position, and I was the one who put you there. And you were right, your family is a bit full on. Well meaning, but—"

"They're wonderful," Anna interjected fiercely, and Simon smiled.

"Absolutely. They're wonderful. I wouldn't say a word

against them, and I admire your father hugely. But… I suppose, in certain situations, they can be a bit full on. I'm only saying I understood what you meant, back at The Bell."

"Thank you," Anna said after a pause. "But I still wish I hadn't told you all that. You're going to look at me differently because of it. You won't be able to help it."

Simon frowned. "How do you think I'm going to look at you?"

She gave a little shake of her head, and then sighed. "Like someone who's broken."

The words pierced Simon right to the core. "We're all broken, Anna. That's the nature of being human. I'm as broken as you are, if not more."

"How?" she demanded. "You seem pretty together, to me."

"We all try to hide it, don't we?" he shot back. "We're not out there, yelling from the rooftops how messed up we are inside, how sad and scared."

"Are you sad and scared?" She sounded dubious.

Simon knew he didn't have any right to hide things from her when she'd told him so much, but it felt like dangerously overloading the front end of their relationship, if he could even say they had one. A friendship, at least, he hoped. Of sorts.

"I have been sad and scared," he said at last. "Even if I'm not feeling that way precisely at this moment."

Anna was silent, staring out the window. "I won't ask

you about that now," she said finally. "Even though I'm curious. But just because I bared my soul doesn't mean you should. It's not tit for tat."

"Thank you," Simon said, feeling both startled and touched because even though he would have told her if she'd asked, he realized he wasn't ready for the same kind of sharing yet.

"But there is something, isn't there?" Anna said quietly. "I mean something specific. Some event or relationship or something, something that's hurt you in some way."

"Yes," he said after a moment. "There is." It felt like a surprisingly big confession.

※»»×«««

KESWICK WAS HEAVING with shoppers and holidaymakers and it took twenty minutes to find a space in one of the town's car parks. The pedestrianised street leading to the Market Square was thronged with people and strung with Christmas lights, with shop windows decorated with ornaments and holly.

"This is certainly putting me in the Christmas spirit," Anna said as they browsed in a craft shop and she inspected some mohair wool for Esther, who had always been a great knitter.

"It certainly is." Simon absently flicked through a book of knitting patterns. They had, by mutual, silent agreement, decided to stay together to shop. Anna had considered offering to split up, which made sense, but she hadn't wanted to and she was glad Simon had chosen to stay with her, even if he had nothing to buy in the craft shop.

"Who are you buying presents for?" she asked as she selected several balls of the mohair and paid for them at the till.

"Not too many people. Your father, for one, and my own parents. I'll send them something touristy, most likely." He gave her a lopsided grin.

"No one else?" Anna asked. It was an even smaller list than her own.

"A friend from theological college who's moved to a curacy in Nottingham. He's married and just had a baby, so I'll most likely buy some revoltingly twee baby gro that says 'Santa's Littlest Helper' or something."

Anna laughed at that. "I'm sure he'll love it."

They strolled out of the shop and back into the busy street. "So, what are you thinking of getting my father? A book on the most beautiful churches in Britain? He's only got three."

Simon gave a wry grimace. "People mean well."

"Yes, I know, but if you know my father at all, you know religious kitsch is definitely not his thing. Although, I have to admit, I've given him a fair share of it over the years. When I was about nine I gave him a paperweight that said 'you have to look through the rain to see the rainbow'."

"He still has it on his desk. And twee as it is, it's also true. But it's good to know I have a lifetime of naff religious gifts to look forward to."

"I promise not to buy you any paperweights," Anna joked, and then blushed, because what she'd said made it sound as if they had some sort of future together, as if she'd be buying presents for him for many Christmases to come.

"That's a relief," Simon said lightly, without any awkwardness, and they continued down the street.

It was remarkably pleasant simply to stroll and browse, chatting about nothing important or even in particular. Comments about gifts, about shops, about Keswick, little jokes and asides, all the conversation Anna, in her anxiety, usually couldn't manage. Why was it suddenly possible, and even easy, with Simon?

Because he already knew her worst and weakest, as he'd said? It was a rather incredible silver lining to that cloud of doom.

They had tea and scones in a tiny little teashop with spindly tables and chairs, their knees inadvertently pressing against each other under the table. In addition to the mohair wool for Esther, Anna had picked up the latest juicy beach read for Rachel, who loved those types of books, and a fleece jumper for her mother, who never seemed to have enough. For her father, she'd bought a moleskin diary for the new year. Simon had bought an assortment of locally made chutneys and jams for his parents, and the promised baby gro for his friend, with "The Littlest Elf" written on the front in red curlicue script.

"So everyone in your family is together for Christmas save for your youngest sister, Miriam," Simon said as they sipped their tea. "What's she like?"

"A bit of a wanderer. A free spirit." A smile of affection tugged at Anna's mouth. "Spoilt, of course, for being the baby, but she doesn't seem to be the worse for it."

"How old is she?"

"Twenty-one. She was a bit of an oops, but we all adore her."

"Your father said she was living in Australia?"

"Yes, for now. You never know where Miriam will turn up next. She took a gap year when she was eighteen, but then she ended up never taking her place at uni. She's always got some job, nannying or waitressing or picking fruit, something to pay the bills as she travels around the globe. She's only been back home twice in all that time, although she Skypes fairly often."

"You all must miss her."

"Yes, we do. My parents worry. I hope she'll come back at some point and settle down, although to what I don't know. I can't picture Miriam working the nine-to-five like the rest of us."

"She sounds like quite the character."

"She's lovely. Warm and full of fun." Anna felt a pang for her sister. "She came and stayed with me in Manchester when she was about sixteen, and we had such a laugh." Miriam was one of the only people who had, on occasion, managed to bring Anna out of herself. "Anyway, I'm sure we'll Skype her on Christmas Day. And of course there's this announcement Mum and Dad are going to make. Who knows what that is." Something in Simon's face made Anna say slowly, "But you do, don't you?"

"I can't say," Simon said and Anna felt a sudden lurch of fear. "Wait, is it serious? I was assuming it was just something random, like they're going to buy goats or a timeshare in Majorca."

"Two very different things," Simon said with a smile.

"Yes, but—" Anna shook her head slowly. "It isn't something like that, is it?"

"Really, Anna, it's not for me to say. I'm sorry."

"You're really freaking me out now." She put her cup back on the saucer with a shaky hand. "No one's… no one's ill, are they?"

"No." Simon looked regretful. "Sorry, I wish I hadn't said anything."

"You didn't."

"I know, but even admitting I know something… it's irritating and upsetting to you. I get that, but I really can't violate your father's confidence."

"Right." She took a deep breath. "They said they were going to tell us on Sunday, after church."

"Then you don't have to wait long."

"Two days." Suddenly it felt like forever. "We should get back," Anna said, looking at the lowering skies. "I fancy getting stuck in Keswick Christmas traffic at nightfall about as much as I do being up a fell then."

"Likewise," Simon said, and rose from the table. He insisted on paying for their teas and Anna decided not to protest. She wanted to recapture some of the easy camaraderie they'd begun to share earlier in the day, but it felt elusive now, with the worry of her father's announcement hanging over her like a cloud, shrouding one of the fells in the distance, misty and cold, obscuring the view.

Back in the car, they sat in Keswick traffic for twenty silent minutes before turning onto the A66. Simon gave her a wry smile. "We seem doomed to awkward oversharing."

"Or not sharing enough," Anna shot back, but she was smiling. She was glad Simon had said something. "Do you think you'll be happy in Thornthwaite?" she asked after they'd driven a few miles in less tense silence, if not precisely companionable.

"I certainly hope so. I'll do my level best to be."

"Still, it can be a lonely place for a single person," Anna said. "It's all young couples and families and empty nesters."

"I imagine I'll be quite busy."

Anna nodded, wondering why she'd bothered to make the observation. Had she been fishing for information? Was Simon single? Did it matter? He lived in Thornthwaite; she lived in Manchester. She could scarcely believe how quickly she'd thought about it, though. The memory of his arms around her, her body leaning into him, flashed through her mind yet again. Was she starting to crush on him simply because he was nice, and she had so little experience? Probably.

"What are you thinking about?" Simon asked, and Anna turned to him with a start.

"What? Why do you ask?"

"Because you looked deep in thought."

"Umm… I don't even know." Her mind had gone completely blank so she couldn't even come up with a credible excuse. "Just zoning, I suppose."

"Right."

Anna willed herself not to flush. *Face, calm down. Do not go scarlet. Do not. Do not.* She felt the colour and heat surge upwards and she looked towards the window. Night was falling, the fells already lost in dusky gloom. It was highly likely Simon didn't think of her that way. Wouldn't consider her romantically in a million years. His training vicar's daughter? A long-distance relationship at the start of a new job? A woman who had already shown herself to be fairly unhinged and anxious? Of course not. She was mad to be entertaining such a notion, even for a second.

By the time Simon had turned into the church lane, it was completely dark and Anna was feeling tired and a little bit dispirited. "Where's your house?" she asked as he parked in front of the vicarage. "Are you staying in the flat off the high street?" Several curates had made that their home.

"Yes, for the moment."

"For the moment?" She raised her eyebrows. "Are you planning on moving?"

"Eventually." Simon sounded evasive. He got out of the car and came around to open her door. "Thanks for coming to Keswick with me."

"Thanks for driving me."

He walked her to the door, just as if it was a date. Just as if he might kiss her at the end, even if just on the cheek.

"I enjoyed the day, Anna," Simon said quietly. "I hope we can do it again."

"Go Christmas shopping in Keswick?" She dared to tease.

"Just spend time together, really," Simon said with an adorably self-conscious smile.

Anna's heart tumbled in her chest. "Th-th-that would be nice." Damn her stammer. Now was not the time.

"Good."

For one heart-stopping second, Anna was sure he was going to kiss her. On the cheek, but still. He leaned forward, and she braced herself, her toes curling inside her boots.

Then the front door was wrenched open, and Rachel stood there, looking shaken and upset. Simon stepped back and Anna stared at her sister in surprise.

"What—" Anna began, but Rachel just shook her head and moved past them, out into the night.

Chapter Eight

"WHAT'S GOING ON with Rachel?"

Anna stood in the doorway of the kitchen, watching her mother fly around, a pot in one hand and a salt shaker in the other. "Can I help?"

"You're back," Ruth exclaimed, banging the pot on the stove. "It's just spaghetti bolognaise for tea, I'm afraid…"

"That's fine, Mum." Anna took the salt shaker out of her hand and filled the pot up with water. "I can do it, if you like. Spag bol is in my limited repertoire. You can sit down, put your feet up."

"I like being busy…" Ruth began, but strangely she looked almost tearful. Anna felt another pang of worry assailed her.

"Is everything all right?" she asked as she rummaged through the fridge for a package of mince.

"Why wouldn't everything be all right?"

Classic Holley, to deflect with a question. "Because you seem a little…" Anna paused, wanting to choose her words with care. "Riled."

"I'm not riled." Ruth sighed. "Just feeling my age, perhaps."

"Your *age?*" Her mother was fifty-nine.

"Or something," Ruth said with a sigh.

"Does it have to do with Dad's announcement? What is that about, anyway?"

"I can hardly tell you before your sisters. You'll find out soon enough, tomorrow night."

"Why tomorrow night?"

"We wanted it after Simon's ordination."

Anna stared at her, mystified. "Why?"

"I can't explain it now. Are you going to put that mince on to fry?"

"Yes." Anna ripped open the package. "If you can't tell me about that, can you at least tell me what's going on with Rachel?"

"Rachel?" Now Ruth was the one sounding mystified. "What about her?"

"She just ran out of the vicarage looking upset."

"Did she? I have no idea why." Ruth's forehead furrowed. "She and Dan had just come in from walking Charlie. I thought she'd be over the moon, now the holidays have properly started."

"Yes…" Had she been imagining how upset Rachel had looked? But she'd brushed by them without a word. There might be a simple explanation, and yet… Anna couldn't help but feel there was more going on than she knew.

She glanced at her mother, who was standing in the middle of the kitchen as if she didn't know what to do. "Are you sure you're all right, Mum?"

"What? I'm fine." Her mother disappeared into the pantry and came back with a stack of plates. "If you're going to make the bolognaise, I'll set the table."

Anna didn't get a chance to talk to Rachel that evening, as she came in right as they were sitting down for supper, and then went back to the shoebox-sized cottage she rented on the high street. Ruth had offered to let her live at home to save money, but Rachel had wanted her own space, just as Esther had, moving out right after uni, even though she'd stayed in the village. Still both of her sisters seemed to spend most of their time at their parents' house, and Anna could understand why.

The vicarage, despite its draughts, was a cosy, welcoming place. She could acknowledge that, enjoy it even, although it was still a hard place to be for her.

After supper, her father asked her to play a board game, and she spent a companionable evening with her parents getting slaughtered at Scrabble.

"Not another seven-letter word," she exclaimed as Ruth lay out her tiles. "That's your third one."

"Your mother is the expert Scrabble player in this family," Roger said with a fond look for his wife. Ruth looked up with a smile. "How many games do you think we've played at this table, in front of the fire?"

"Hundreds," Ruth said softly, and they exchanged a look that seemed to mean more than Anna could fathom.

Would she ever have that one day? A whole shared history of little moments in life, games and jokes and laughter, along with the bigger stuff—the milestones, the birthdays, the sorrows and joys? Her mind flitted to Simon and she banished the thought. She barely knew him. It was silly to be thinking that way.

The next day was Saturday, two days before Christmas Eve, and Ruth enlisted Anna's help from the moment she got up to help clean the house, make the evening meal, and generally get the vicarage ready for Christmas. Anna gathered fresh holly to decorate the mantelpieces, and made an extra batch of shortbread because her mother was worried they wouldn't have enough. She hoovered the downstairs twice, because Charlie shed all over the hall carpet before lunch, and then took him for a walk before banishing him to the entrance hall where he stared at her balefully through the glass-paned door.

The wardens were coming over for their pre-Christmas sherry that evening, and then there was the big Sunday dinner with her father's announcement tomorrow. On Christmas Eve, they had the Sunday school for a Christingle-making party before the service, and then of course all the fuss of Christmas itself. Anna wondered, not for the first time, how her mother managed it all.

On Sunday morning, the church was full to bursting,

which was unusual, since the regular attenders numbered in the dozens rather than the hundreds. Christmas bulked the numbers up, and of course there was Simon's ordination with the bishop preaching the sermon.

Anna dressed carefully, wearing the burgundy knit dress she'd been intending for the Christmas Day service, and pulling her dark hair back into a low bun. She was being silly, she knew that; Simon would be so busy with the service, he probably wouldn't even notice her.

Lots of other people did, though, and Anna made her way monosyllabically through the well-meaning parishioners who wanted to hear about her life in Manchester, and why she didn't come home more often, and what did she think about Dan and Rachel? Anna's palms went damp and her heart raced and she forced out smiles and single words—as ever, it was all she could manage.

She finally found her way to the pew where her sisters and their significant others were already seated, unable to keep from giving a gusty sight of relief.

Rachel gave her a sympathetic smile. "It's a bit like running the gauntlet, isn't it?"

Anna just nodded. Rachel chatted with everyone, words, smiles, and even hugs were all so easy for her to give. And yet her sister looked a little strained right now, lines of tension bracketing her eyes and mouth.

"Rach"—Anna leaned over to whisper—"are you okay?"

Rachel gave her a startled glance. "Of course I am. Why

wouldn't I be?" Her sister sounded so surprised that Anna decided she must have been imagining Rachel's angst yesterday. Maybe she'd just been in a rush.

She turned to face the front of the church, with its soaring, arched ceiling and the magnificent stained glass window that was seven hundred years old. Then the service started, and everyone rose for the first hymn and the procession of the choir and clergy.

It gave her a pang to see Simon at the front, standing next to her father, in his black clerical robes and the stiff white dog collar. Somehow, when they'd been shopping in Keswick or sipping tea or climbing down a fell she'd half-forgotten he was a curate. A priest.

It was impossible to forget now, with the service taking place, the organ music and the bishop's important tones reminding her how special this all was. And then Simon was kneeling and making vows, and the bishop anointed him with oil. Anna had seen this type of service before, with her father's other curates, but it felt different now. It felt more important, because she actually cared about Simon.

Was it just because he knew so much about her? Maybe spilling all her secrets had created a false sense of intimacy. Maybe she really was being completely ridiculous.

Anna glanced down the pew at Esther and Will, Rachel and Dan, and a pang of sorrowful envy assailed her heart. She'd been alone her whole life, in one way or another, and she was tired of it. She'd never been brave enough to embark on a romantic relationship, and she wasn't sure if she was now, but it was nice to dream. And perhaps that was all it was… dreams.

The service ended, and Anna made her way through the gauntlet at the back; someone had brought champagne and Christmas cake and Anna dutifully took a glass and slice, knowing to slip out as she longed to would be rude. Fortunately, with her mouth full of cake, she had an excuse for not talking.

Then Simon was in front, smiling ruefully. "You don't think of me differently, do you?" he asked, tugging at his clerical collar.

Anna swallowed a mouthful of cake, practically choking on a sultana. "Sort of," she admitted. "I don't mean to."

"Your father warned me that people look at you differently when you're in this garb. It can be a good thing in some situations, but not-so-good in others."

"And what is it with me?" Anna asked as she wondered what they were talking about.

"I suppose," Simon said slowly, "that's up to you." A smile unfurled across his face and made excitement leap in Anna's belly. It felt as if there was a significant subtext to this conversation, and she was afraid to hope what it was.

"Shall I call you Father Simon now?" she joked, and Simon pretended to shudder.

"Please don't. I'll have enough of the parish wanting to do that, and I don't feel like I'm anyone's father."

"But, you know, you have the spiritual wisdom and all that."

"I'm not sure I've got much of that," Simon said and, for a second, a bleakness came over his face that Anna recognized from when they'd been up on the fell. He had some story, some secret, and she longed to know what it was. "I think we're going back to the vicarage now," Simon said. "Esther's giving me a rather beady look."

"That's just Esther," Anna said, but she followed Simon out of the church and across to the vicarage.

The house was full of delicious smells and toasty warm from the fires blazing in four different hearths. Her mother bustled out from the kitchen; she must have nipped out of church the minute the service ended.

"Dinner's almost ready. Anna, pour Simon a sherry. Or should I say the reverend?" She gave him an affectionate look and Anna fetched the bottle of Harvey's Bristol Cream they'd picked up from Booth's yesterday.

"This is all very civilized," Simon remarked as Anna took one of her mother's crystal sherry glasses from the china cupboard in the dining room. The table had been laid magnificently with a snowy linen table cloth and crimson napkins, her mother's Christmas china and a centrepiece of holly and ivy that Anna had helped to fashion.

"It is, isn't it? My mother loves to entertain."

"A busy vicarage is a happy place," Simon said. He glanced at her when she didn't reply. "Isn't it?"

"Yes, generally."

"Did you find it hard, having people coming in and out all the time?'

"Not hard, exactly. Just…" She concentrated on pouring the sherry. "Sometimes it felt like it was easy to be missed, I suppose, but that wasn't always a bad thing. Here you are." She smiled at him as she handed him his glass of sherry, the amber liquid glinting in the light.

"Thank you." Simon took a sip of sherry, his warm, hazel gaze on her. "I'm glad you're here, Anna."

Anna's insides did a funny little tumble and suddenly she found it hard to speak, for an entirely new reason. She nodded once, unable to think of how to reply. "I should start the Yorkshire puddings. That's always been my job."

Back in the steamy busyness of the kitchen Anna focused on stirring the Yorkshire pudding batter to an airy froth. What had Simon meant exactly, that he was glad she was here? Had it been a throwaway comment, the kind of thing a curate would say to a parishioner, little more than "good to see you"? Anna didn't think so, but she was afraid to hope. Afraid to want, and to dream.

"I think you've stirred that batter enough," Ruth remarked. "Your head is in the clouds today, I think."

"SORRY," ANNA MURMURED. She reached for a muffin pan

and began spooning a bit of oil in each cup. Esther came in, bearing an impressive triple tier chocolate cake.

"Pudding," she announced, and Ruth made a fuss of the cake while Anna put the Yorkshires in the Aga.

She spent the next half hour helping her mother and sisters get dinner on the table; her mother had outdone herself with a huge joint of roast beef and all the trimmings.

"And we just had a roast dinner a few day ago," Rachel said with a smile for her mum. "You spoil us."

"You can never have too many roast dinners," Roger replied. They all sat down, the table groaning with food, and as soon as grace had been said, her parents exchanged a strange, tense look.

"So?" Esther prompted as she loaded up her plate. "What's this announcement, Dad?"

"Because we've got an announcement too," Will said, and Esther shot him a quelling look.

"And we do as well," Dan pitched in and when Anna looked at Rachel, she was biting her lip. "What was going on?"

"Well, I don't have any announcements," she said, and Simon gave her a quick, affectionate smile that made her tingle.

"Right. Well, perhaps you two ought to go first, then. Esther? Will? What's your announcement?"

"I'm not sure now is the—" Esther began, but Will cut her off.

"Esther's pregnant," he said proudly. "The baby's due in six months."

"Oh, Esther!" Tears sparkled on Ruth's lashes as she rose to give her eldest a hug. "That's such wonderful, wonderful news. I'm so thrilled!"

"As am I, of course," Roger said genially, and went to kiss Esther on the cheek. "You must both be so excited."

"Yes, we are," Esther said, but she didn't look excited.

"Have you been feeling terribly ill?" Ruth asked. "I thought you looked a bit peaky…"

As Ruth grilled her on the kind of pregnancy details Anna really didn't need to know, she turned to Rachel. "What's your news, then?"

"Oh, I don't—" Rachel began half-heartedly, and Dan reached over to put an arm around her.

"Why not share our happiness?" he said and, after a second, Rachel nodded. Dan looked up at everyone. "I'm pleased to say I've asked Rachel to be my wife, and she's accepted."

Cue another round of exclamations and kisses. Anna gave her sister a hug, wondering why she didn't look more pleased. Both Esther and Rachel seemed less than thrilled about their news, but perhaps it was just nerves. And, as for her, the only one without a milestone on the horizon? Anna met Simon's gaze and he gave her a rueful smile that felt as good as a hug.

It was as if he'd just said, "I know, everyone's got something going on. It's a little bit lonely, isn't it? I feel it too." She smiled back, and for a second it was as if the whole room, with all its noise and people, fell away and it was just her and Simon, smiling.

"So, Dad, now it's your turn. What's your news?"

"Well." Roger dabbed his mouth with his napkin as he exchanged a quick, questioning look with Ruth, who nodded. "I wish Miriam could be here for this, but we'll Skype her later."

"Sounds important," Esther murmured.

"It's nothing as exciting as what you two have planned, but, after a lot of thought and discussion and prayer, your mother and I have decided it's time for me to retire from being vicar of Thornthwaite."

A thunderclap of astounded silence greeted this announcement. Everyone stared.

"Retire," Esther said. "But you're only sixty."

"I know, and I don't intend to simply keel over or collect seashells. I've accepted another position. It starts in July."

"Another position." Now it was Rachel who sounded utterly incredulous. "You mean you're going to move?"

"Yes." Roger paused, looking determined, regretful, and excited all at once. "I've accepted a position in Jinan."

"Jinan?" Rachel boggled. "Where is that?"

"China," Esther said flatly.

"That's right." Roger beamed at her, as if she'd just answered a pub quiz question correctly. "I've accepted a position helping house churches in the city. It's something very different and challenging, which is what I wanted."

Anna could hardly believe. Her father was leaving his sleepy village in the Lake District where he'd spent the last thirty years, to move to China? Was he having a mid-life crisis twenty years late?

"I can see you're all surprised," Roger said quietly. "But as I said before, your mother and I have thought long and hard about this. I have ten years or less until retirement, and I want to do something different. Something useful. Besides, I'm tired of bickering with my congregation about whether we should exchange the pews for chairs."

That, Anna knew, was a battle that had been going on for a decade at least. Still… China.

No one said anything for a long moment, the only sound the crackle and pop of the logs settling in the fire.

Then Rachel said forlornly, "But we're all here."

"I know," Roger said gently. "And obviously that doesn't have to change. We'll come back for visits. And you can all come see us in China."

"But…" Rachel's eyes were huge in her pale face. "It's not the same."

"No," Roger agreed, and he sounded genuinely regretful. "But it might be better for you and Esther if we're not here. Spread your wings a bit without being the vicar's children."

"But…" Rachel swallowed hard. "I wanted to get married in the church, with you officiating."

"And so you can. Nothing need change that."

"But July… that's only six months away!" Rachel looked tearful, and Anna knew it wasn't just about her wedding. Her parents moving out of the vicarage, all the way to China… it was too big to take in.

"Even if I'm somewhere else, I can still officiate the wedding," Roger said gently. "You don't need to worry about that, darling."

"But there will be another vicar here," Rachel said, sounding as if she just couldn't believe it. "What if he—or she—won't allow it?"

"That won't happen."

"The position will be vacant for a year, won't it?" Esther said. She sat tight-lipped, her arms folded. "There will be an interregnum."

"Actually, there won't," Roger said. "I've managed to arrange it to have someone take over from me immediately, to cause the least amount of disruption."

"Someone?" Esther looked suspicious. "And the parish agreed? The wardens and everyone?"

"Yes, they're thrilled."

"Who is it?" Rachel asked, and Anna felt a strange, trembling sensation inside as she braced herself for her father's answer.

"Why, it's Simon, of course."

Chapter Nine

I T WAS CHRISTMAS Eve. Anna woke up and blinked at the ceiling, the dull, grey light of a winter's morning barely illuminating her bedroom. Yesterday's conversation, with all its unexpected revelations, filtered through her mind. Esther, pregnant. Rachel, engaged. Her father, retired. And Simon… Simon was going to be the new vicar of Thornthwaite.

"You've known all along, haven't you?" Anna asked when they were alone in the kitchen, clearing up. She tried not to sound accusing, although some small part of her felt strangely betrayed.

"Yes, of course I have." Simon scraped a plate into the bin and threw a piece of gristly meat into Charlie's bowl. "It was part of the reason for the delay in my ordination."

"Why didn't you tell me?" Anna asked even though she knew the answer.

"It wasn't my secret to tell." Simon looked at her seriously. "It's obviously a shock to you and your sisters, but do you mind?"

"Mind?" Anna shook her head slowly. "Why should I

mind you taking over? I'd rather it was you than some stranger."

"I'm glad you don't think of me as a stranger."

"Of course I don't," Anna said, and blushed. "But I can't imagine my parents not being here... it seems impossible. And you... you'll live in the vicarage?" Her chest went tight at the thought. She might have avoided Thornthwaite for the last few years, but this was her home.

"Yes," Simon agreed quietly. "I will."

"You'll rattle around this place by yourself."

"I know."

"You should get married and have a load of children to fill it up," she said recklessly, and Simon gave her a funny, crooked smile.

"I'd love that."

Anna could not think how to reply.

Now she swung her legs up and gazed out the window at the stark, leafless trees silhouetted against a heavy grey sky. Esther had maintained a stony silence for the rest of yesterday, and Rachel had gone quiet, often looking as if she were on the brink of tears. Simon had left soon after dinner had finished, and the whole day had ended on a rather damp squib. Perhaps today would feel more festive. Perhaps not.

Anna dressed and went downstairs, stopping short when she saw her mother sitting at the kitchen table, cradling a cup of coffee and looking pensive and a little bit sad.

"Mum?"

"Hello, darling." Ruth looked up with a quick, distracted smile. "There's cinnamon buns in the warming oven."

"You made cinnamon buns?" Anna shook her head, smiling. "You never stop."

"We always have cinnamon buns on Christmas Eve." Ruth bit her lip, and Anna sat down across from her mother.

"How are you feeling about this move, Mum?" she asked gently. "China… it's a really big step."

"Yes." Her mother let out a rather shuddery sigh. "It's always been your father's dream, to go overseas. It's such important work."

"Yes, but… is it your dream?"

Ruth sighed again, this time a more pragmatic, accepting sound. "A marriage is full of compromises, Anna. This was my dream." She gestured to the cosy kitchen with its oak table, the bright Aga with Charlie sprawled in front of it, all the comfortably shabby trappings of a village life. "To live here, to raise my children…" Her lips trembled and Anna knew instinctively she was thinking about Jamie.

"Mum…" She reached out a hand and Ruth clasped it tightly, surprising her.

Her mother always seemed so busy and self-sufficient, but in that moment Anna felt her mum needed her. She squeezed her mother's hand and Ruth gave her a grateful, if tearful, smile.

"There have been hard moments along the way, goodness knows. Some very hard moments." She pressed her lips together. "But I've loved it here, and I've been so very thankful for our years here."

"But then don't you want to stay?"

"It's possible to want two different things at the same time. I want to stay, but I also want to make your father happy. He's been feeling restless for a few years now, hearing the call to a new place, a different place. I know being in Jinan will be very invigorating for him. And for me." Her smile turned wry. "Although it might take me longer to get used to it."

"And what about Rachel's wedding? And Esther's baby?"

"We'll be here for both those events. I admit, I'd rather see my grandchild grow up every day, but I don't think we'll be in Jinan forever. This is something your father needs to do after thirty years of village life, and I understand that. I accept it."

Anna felt a wave of tender love for her mother, as well as heartfelt admiration. Ruth Holley had given her life to the village and church, serving in every way imaginable, cooking, cleaning, teaching Sunday school and leading toddler groups, always with a smile, and now she was going to give it all up for the man she loved, and the marriage she honoured.

"I think you're amazing, Mum," Anna said quietly, and Ruth let out a shaky laugh.

"Thank you, my darling. I don't feel very amazing. I feel quite ordinary, muddling through as best as I can, but thank you." She squeezed Anna's hand back. "And what about you?

How are you feeling about all these announcements?"

"A bit like I've been left out," Anna admitted.

After her mother had been so honest, she felt she needed to be as well. She wanted to, because she'd never had this kind of open conversation with her mother before. In truth, she hadn't been sure either of them were capable of it.

"I don't have any major life events happening. No change of job, no husband or boyfriend, and certainly no baby."

"I must say, I'm pleased about the baby. But as for the rest…" Her mother looked almost sly. "Are you sure there's no one on the horizon?"

Heat stole through Anna's cheeks as she tried to meet her mother's gaze and failed. "I don't think so," she murmured. "Not really."

"Not really?" Her mother sounded pleased Anna had admitted that much.

"I don't know," Anna answered, and that felt as if she were admitting even more. "What can I do to help get ready for Christmas?" she asked brightly in a glaringly obvious attempt to change the subject.

Ruth laughed fondly. "Oh, my darling. I do hope the horizon looms closer than you might even realize. As for Christmas… would you mind terribly if I asked you to clean the downstairs bathroom? With the wardens coming over for their sherry…"

"Of course." Impulsively, Anna leaned over and kissed

her mother's cheek.

She wasn't used to offering demonstrations of physical affection but, in that moment, she felt the need as well as the desire to. Her mother was a wonderful woman, and even though Anna had purposely stayed away these last few years, she'd always loved her and missed her. And, Anna realized, despite all her anxieties, she was glad to be back in Thornthwaite.

She spent the morning scrubbing and cleaning, and then in the quiet lull of the afternoon when her mother was having a rest and her father was looking over his Christmas Eve sermon, she decided to walk over to the curate's flat.

It felt like a move of unparalleled daring, at least for her, but Anna was determined. She'd dreaded coming back to Thornthwaite but, amazingly, she found a small part of her confidence had been restored—thanks to Simon. Telling him her secrets *had* liberated her, even if the prospect was still rather terrifying.

She slipped out of the vicarage without telling anyone where she was going; she'd be back in time for the special evening meal they always had on Christmas Eve, shepherd's pie to remember the shepherds who followed the star on that holy night, followed by her mother's chocolate mousse pie, simply because it was delicious.

The curates of Thornthwaite had always lived in a flat up on Finkle Street, in a tall, terraced house owned by the diocese. The top two floors were rented to tenants and the ground floor was reserved for a curate, when there was one. Anna had only been in the flat a handful of times over the years, when one curate or another had invited the vicar's family over for tea crowded into the small sitting room, cups balanced precariously on knees.

Now she stood in front of the door of peeling red paint, a tarnished brass knocker in the shape of a lion grinning at her, daring her to do it. Knock. Enter.

"Anna!" Simon's surprise morphed into a smile of genuine delight as he answered the knock she'd finally, after a few minutes, dared to give, lifting the knocker and dropping it with an echoing thud.

"I hope I'm not interrupting anything…" Already she was feeling the weight of her nerves, the anxious beat of her heart.

"Of course not. Come in, come in." Simon stepped aside so she could enter the tiny entrance hall with its ancient flocked wallpaper and floor of cracked Victorian tile, everything overlaid with a dated 1980s refurbishment.

"This place has seen better days, hasn't it?" she remarked as Simon led her through to the small sitting room with its wildly patterned carpet.

"Yes, the diocese keeps promising to update it but nothing's happened yet."

"I suppose it doesn't matter much to you, since you'll be moving soon."

"Perhaps, but the next curate will suffer headache from

all the clashing plaids." The smile he gave her was already wonderfully familiar, lopsided and endearing. "Let me get you something to drink."

"All right." The nervousness she'd felt at coming here, at presuming, was slowly starting to abate, like the receding of a tide. "Thank you."

"And let me take your coat." He leapt forward to do so, his hands coming onto her shoulders. They spent a humorously awkward moment with Simon trying to help her struggle out of her coat as her arms got caught up in the sleeves. By the time he'd finally relieved her of her parka, they were both breathless and blushing.

"Sorry about that," Simon muttered, and went to hang her coat in the hall.

Anna paced the little room, already feeling her apprehension return. What was she doing here? What did she want? She glanced down at the gift she'd bought, wondering if it was ridiculous. She doubted Simon had bought her a gift. They barely knew each other. And yet…

"A glass of wine?" Simon asked as he came back into the room. His hair was mussed in its usual way, and he wore a pair of faded jeans and a jumper with holes in the elbows. His eyes were warm and glinting and he looked wonderful.

"Yes, please, preferably not mulled."

He laughed at that. "You've had your share for the season?"

"And then some. I do like it, but Mum makes it by the

vat."

"Be back in a tick." He disappeared into the kitchen and returned with a bottle of pinot noir. "It's not posh, but I hope it will do."

"It's lovely, thanks." She thrust the box she'd been holding at him. "I brought you this."

"Oh—a present?" He looked both surprised and pleased.

"Just something small. For, you know, your ordination."

"Thank you. That's so kind." He took the box, gazing down at with something like wonder. Anna gave an uncertain laugh.

"Well, open it, then."

"All right." She fidgeted while he did, fighting the urge to explain the gift, which seemed silly. Perhaps she should have given him something solemn and leather-bound, rather than a gift that was more like a joke.

Simon lifted the two mugs. "'Keep Calm and Pray'," he read on the first. "And 'More Tea, Vicar?'" he finished on the second. "They're perfect."

"I thought you could start up a collection of religious kitsch."

"These are not kitschy at all," he demurred, his eyes sparkling. "Really, I was half-expecting something in stained glass. Shall we christen them?"

"You mean with the wine?"

"Why not?"

Simon opened the bottle with a satisfying pop and then

poured generous measures into the two mugs, handing one to Anna.

"This won't make you tiddly for the midnight service?" she teased, and Simon shook his head.

"Even if it does, I'm only standing up front looking vaguely important. Your father is giving the sermon." He paused, his mug in one hand. "Will you be there?"

"Yes. The midnight carol service is one of my favourites."

"Cheers, then." He hefted his mug and they clinked china before Simon gestured for her to sit on the faded, overstuffed sofa. "So, how are things up at the vicarage, in the wake of all the family news?"

"Okay, I think. I haven't seen Rachel or Esther since yesterday, though."

"They seemed to be hit hard by your father's retirement."

"It affects them more, living here."

"And what do you think about it?"

Anna sighed and tucked her knees up under her as she took a sip of wine. "I'm surprised, but I'm also glad for my father," she said slowly. "He's so jolly and cheerful about everything, but when he was talking yesterday I suddenly had the sense that he'd been stagnating here for a while. It was strange."

"I think he's ready for something new," Simon agreed, and she glanced at him.

"What about you? How do you feel about becoming the next vicar?"

"Nervous. Hopeful." She didn't think she'd ever get tired of his lopsided smile. "I've wanted to live in a small community, a place where you can really know people, where you can help them."

"Is that why you decided to go into ministry? To help people?"

"Yes, it seemed like the best way to do it. Minister to their souls along with their bodies."

"You sound like my dad."

"He's a great man."

"You won't get tired of it? All the baptisms and funerals and squabbles over pews or hymns? Sometimes it all seems appallingly tedious."

"That's life, though, isn't it?"

"I suppose."

"What about you?" Simon asked after a moment. "Do you think you'll stay in Manchester for the long term?" The question, so casually asked, still seemed weighted with extra meaning.

"I don't know," Anna said slowly.

"You're happy there?"

Happy? The word jolted her unexpectedly and, to Anna's horror, tears welled in her eyes. No, no, no. She didn't want to cry.

"Anna?" Simon prompted gently, and she knew he could see the tears she desperately didn't want to shed.

"Sorry." She drew a quick, shuddery breath and dashed

her eyes on her sleeve, hoping to stave off a full-on sob. "Everything's been a bit emotional, with Dad's retirement and coming back here. I haven't been back for Christmas since my uni days."

"What have you done at Christmas instead?"

"Gone out with friends in Manchester. One year my friend and I booked an all-inclusive holiday in Tenerife that was wretched. Sometimes I've just worked."

"Why," Simon asked gently, "have you been avoiding Christmas at home?"

"Because, like I told you before, it's hard to be here."

"But Christmas in particular?"

She paused, startled by his perception. "Jamie loved Christmas," she confessed quietly. "He was so hyper, so full of boy energy. It drove us all mad, but when it—he—was gone. The vicarage felt so very empty. That first Christmas without him… it was awful." She shook her head slowly, willing the tears that still threatened back. "It will be twenty years in April. I shouldn't be this affected still."

"I don't think you ever get over grief," Simon said quietly. "You learn to live with it, but it stays a part of you."

Anna looked up at him, noticing the stark lines of sadness on his face. "You're speaking from experience."

"Yes."

"This is the thing, isn't it?" she asked. "That you mentioned when we were driving to Keswick."

Simon hesitated, and Anna searched his face, looking for

clues. He looked so bleak it made her hart.

"Yes," he said at last.

"Will you…" She paused, realizing she was asking something important and intimate. "Will you tell me about it?"

Simon gazed at her for a moment, still looking so sad that Anna felt a tremor of fear. She longed to help him, to comfort him, but with the grief etched so clearly on his face she wondered if she could. What did she have to offer anyone in terms of solace? She was still so trapped in her own pain and guilt.

"Yes," Simon said at last. "I will."

Chapter Ten

SIMON HAD SERIOUS reservations about burdening Anna with his own emotional pain so early in their friendship, but she deserved his trust along with his honesty, and he wanted to give her both. Still, it was hard.

"First, more wine," he said with a wry smile, and topped up both their mugs.

"You don't have to tell me, if you don't want to," Anna said quickly. "I know how hard it is to share personal stuff. You know I know." She smiled ruefully, the sheen of tears from her own grief still in her wide blue eyes. "I don't want to presume anything. We barely know each other."

Simon arched an eyebrow. "We barely know each other?" he repeated lightly, trying not to show how surprisingly hurt he was by that casual remark. "I don't think that's exactly true."

"No, but…" Anna bit her lip. "I didn't mean it quite like that. Only that we haven't known each other for very long."

And yet he felt like he'd known her forever, or near enough. It startled and unsettled him, to realize just how much he'd come to enjoy her presence, how alarming he found the prospect of her returning to Manchester and then relegating him to the horrible family friend status, handshakes and chitchat after a Sunday service when she was home—except of course she wouldn't be coming home, because her parents wouldn't be here and the vicarage wouldn't be her home. It would be his.

"Simon?" Anna prompted, looking concerned.

"Sorry, I was miles away for a moment." He rubbed a hand over his face. "I lost someone I loved very much a few years ago," he said, deciding to start with the plain, hard facts. "My fiancée, in fact."

"Oh, no. I'm so sorry." Anna's face was soft with sadness, her eyes wide and dark.

"We'd been engaged for several years." He paused, debating how much to reveal. He wanted to be honest with Anna, but he also wanted to be respectful of Ellie's memory. "I suppose, looking back, that should have been a warning sign. Ellie, my fiancée, kept changing the date of our wedding, pushing it back. She told me she wanted to get married, but everything had to be perfect. And she went through periods of…" He paused. "Of questioning everything. Of questioning me. She was diagnosed with bipolar disorder when she was twenty-one, a year after we'd started dating. We met our second year in uni, and I asked her to marry me on our graduation. It all seemed perfect, except of course it wasn't. Nothing is."

"I'm sorry," Anna said quietly. "I feel like that's all I can say, but it doesn't seem enough. It must have been so very difficult."

"It was." Simons hesitated, knowing he needed to tell her the whole story and yet resisting the emotional gutting of reliving those terrible moments and days. Even now he could see Ellie's face, pale and desperate, begging him to help her and yet he couldn't.

"Ellie really struggled with her condition," He resumed after a moment, choosing each word with care. "She hated going on medication, but she needed it. She felt like a failure, but she wasn't." His throat had started going tight as he remembered the battles they'd had over her prescription pills, how he'd beg her to take them and she'd refuse, screaming at him that if he loved her he wouldn't make her take them. "The medication made her feel numb," he explained to Anna. "She said it was like... like being dead inside." He forced himself to meet her compassionate gaze. "And she'd rather experience the lows as well as the highs than nothing at all."

"I suppose," Anna said after a moment, "I can understand that."

"Yes, I could as well. At least I tried to, but some of her lows... were really low." He swallowed hard. "And it was frightening, to see her so sad and depressed."

"Oh, Simon." Anna leaned over and rested a hand on top of hers.

"I felt helpless a lot of the time," he continued, "but I also sometimes felt annoyed. Angry, even. It felt like she was being selfish. I know that isn't really fair—"

"Nothing about this situation sounds fair."

"No, I suppose not. Life isn't fair, is it? And no one ever said it would be." He sighed, deciding he needed to finish telling her all the bad bits. "Four years ago, Ellie went through a really bad patch. I was so worried about her, but maybe not worried enough." He met Anna's gaze, her face looking so sorrowful and lovely, and said the worst of it. "She killed herself."

Anna gasped softly. "Oh, Simon…"

"An overdose. I was the one who found her." He closed his eyes briefly, remembering the sight of her lifeless body on her bed, her head lolling back against the pillow. "I'd been coming over to pick her up for dinner with her parents. To discuss wedding plans." He drew a shuddering breath. "I called 999, and they were brilliant, they came quickly, took her to A&E, pumped her stomach, did everything they could. But it was too late. She slipped into a coma and then she died five days later."

Anna squeezed his hand. "I can't imagine how hard that must have been."

"But you can, can't you? Because you know what it is to lose someone. Maybe not to feel like it's your fault—"

"It wasn't your fault, Simon."

"I know she had a mental illness, I understand that logically, I really do. But I was the most important person in her life at that time. She loved me, she depended on me, and I can't help but feel that I let her down. I did let her down."

"It wasn't your responsibility to keep her alive."

"Wasn't it?" Simon looked at her bleakly, compelled to more honesty than he'd ever offered anyone before. "I was planning to marry her. I should have been more diligent, more determined, to help her get the help she needed. There's no way around that, Anna."

"Blaming yourself can't help," Anna said softly. "Guilt is the most awful emotion, Simon, especially when it's coupled with regret."

She looked so sad Simon felt a whisper of apprehension. "You almost sound as if you're speaking from experience."

Anna was silent for a long moment. "I suppose," she finally said, "in a way, I am."

❊❊❊

SHE HADN'T MEANT to tell him about Jamie, about her part in his death, and yet now that Simon had unburdened himself so much she felt she had to. She *wanted* to. Maybe it would help.

"Jamie died when he was hit by a car right on Thornthwaite's high street." Her heart started to pound, her throat going tight, her tongue feeling thick as she forced the words out. "It was g-g-g-going too fast. I *know* that."

Simon cocked his head, his warm, thoughtful gaze sweeping slowly over her. "But?" he prompted softly.

"But Jamie ran into the street because he was ch-ch-chasing me." Somehow she managed to get the words out. "We were on our way to school, Mum was behind with Miriam, who was only two. She told us to s-s-s-slow down, but it was s-s-s-such a w-w-w-warm day." She was stammering more than she had in a long time, reliving that awful, awful moment, suspended forever in time in her mind.

The squeal of the car's brakes. The dull thud of the car hitting Jamie's body. Turning around, the laughter still bubbling up in her chest, to see his body fly through the air and then land on the pavement with a terrible, sickening thud.

"He was s-s-s-so s-s-s-still," she whispered, and then found she couldn't talk at all.

Somehow, she was gathered up in Simon's arms as he pulled her close to his chest, her cheek resting against the comforting and steady beat of his heart. He smelled of old-fashioned aftershave and spicy wine. "It wasn't your fault, Anna. It was the car, just as it was Ellie's illness."

"B-b-b-but if I hadn't been running…"

"And if the car hadn't been there, going too fast." He sighed, a sad breath of sound. "The driver must struggle with guilt, as well."

"It was a woman on her way to work. I remember, she was devastated."

"I'm sure." Simon was silent for a moment, stroking her hair as she cuddled into him, craving the security of his embrace. "What point does guilt serve?" he asked finally, his voice quiet and sad. "To make us aware of our mistakes and failings, yes, but then surely we must move on. There is no point being mired in guilt. It only destroys us."

"How do you move on? How do you let yourself?"

"I think it's a choice you have to live out every day. But it can also be a gift, a sudden sense of peace in your soul…"

"Have you felt that?" Anna asked. "Have you moved on?"

"Sometimes I feel as if I have. But on some days, when the memories are coming at me, I don't." He sighed again. "Like I said, it's a choice, a battle, you face every day."

And one she'd been losing. Back in Manchester, she could sometimes make herself forget about her part in Jamie's death, but, here in Thornthwaite, in the vicarage with the love of her parents feeling wonderful and suffocating at the same time? It all came rushing back, overwhelming her, making her feeling as if she were drowning in it.

"You told me before your social anxiety and stammering started after Jamie's death," Simon said slowly. "But it's not just that, is it? It's the guilt you feel."

"Nobody's ever said anything," Anna whispered. She clenched her eyes shut but a tear still trickled out. "We talk about Jamie sometimes, we remember him, but no one has said anything about the day of his death. How it could have been avoided."

Simon eased back so he could look her in the face. Anna's eyes fluttered open, her heart tripping in her chest at the intent look on Simon's face. Gently, he wiped the tear from her cheek with his thumb, and the whisper of his skin against hers made her ache.

"Anna," he asked quietly, his thumb still resting on her cheek, "do you think your family blames you? Is that what you're afraid of?"

It was a question that had lurked like some dark, poisonous cloud on the fringes of her mind, but she'd never let it take over. Never let herself voice it, because to do so would have been to give in, to be lost in that darkness, and never find her way out. But somehow, now, Simon's asking it felt like a bit of light breaking in, the opposite of what she would have expected.

"Yes," she whispered. "I suppose I do."

"Then you need to talk to them about it. I could reassure you and tell you that I know they don't think that, but you need to hear it from them."

"I can't," Anna said, the word a fractured sound. "I can't."

"I understand how you feel that way. I felt like I couldn't talk to Ellie's parents… facing them after I found her, telling them she'd killed herself… it was one of the hardest things I've ever done, but it was also one of the best. Because then we could grieve together, to share the pain. And I think one of the reasons you're so bogged down by this is because you haven't shared it. You haven't grieved with your family properly."

As soon as Simon said the words, Anna knew he was right. It settled into her very bones, along with an ache of yearning. She wanted to share her grief with her family, but how? What if she saw the knowledge in her parents and sisters' eyes? What if they did blame her?

"They don't," Simon said softly, and Anna let out a shaky laugh.

"How did you know what I was thinking?"

"I'm not sure. I just did." He tucked a strand of hair behind her ear, his fingers skimming her cheek, making her shiver. "I feel as if I've known you a long time."

Awareness rippled goose bumps along her skin. "I feel as if I've known you a long time, as well." She looked up at him, a tremor of excitement going through her at the sudden heat she saw in his eyes. The attraction she'd felt wasn't one-sided as she'd feared. Simon felt it too.

His fingers skimmed her cheek again. Anna's heart bumped in her chest. She'd been kissed precisely two times before, both sloppy and slightly unpleasant affairs at the end of a date. She'd never been kissed properly, tenderly, and she wanted to be so now. She wanted to be kissed by Simon.

He was looking at her with the familiar, steady warmth, his fingers resting on her cheek, and Anna's heart was starting to beat like some wild thing locked in a cage. How did these moments *work?* Should she lean closer? Close her eyes? What if she'd got it completely wrong and he didn't want to kiss her at all?

"I don't know if now is the right moment," Simon said in a slightly hoarse voice. "Considering all the heavy things we've just talked about. But the truth is, Anna, I'd really like to kiss you."

Relief burst through her like joyous birdsong. Much better to simply state the truth than play at signals. Much more Simon. "I… I'd like you to kiss me," she whispered.

"Are you sure?" Simon's expression was grave. "Because I know we've just had a very emotional conversation, and I feel like a kiss is kind of a serious thing for both of us."

"You mean you know I don't go around kissing lots of blokes," Anna said with a little laugh. She remembered her drunken confession about having barely been kissed, and she knew Simon remembered it, as well.

"And I don't go around kissing a lot of women," Simon answered. "In fact, I've only kissed two other women in my whole life."

"And I've only kissed two men."

"So we're even."

"In number of people if not number of kisses."

"Should we make a graph?" Out came his wonderfully lopsided smile.

"I think maybe," Anna said, "you should just kiss me."

And so he did, bending his head so his lips brushed hers

in a slow, questioning sweep. Excitement zinged through her, along with a rush of something else—something warm and safe, as opposed to the physical thrill she was definitely feeling, as well. It was as if her heart was saying *yes, you, at last*, even as her body was crying out, *more, please. More, more.*

Simon's hand came down to rest on her shoulder as he deepened the kiss, slowly, questioningly, giving her ample opportunity to back off or break away. But she didn't. Her heart was hammering and a thousand sensations and thoughts were exploding through her mind and body, but she didn't want this kiss to end.

But then it did, after several exquisite minutes, as Simon broke away with a ragged breath. His cheeks were flushed, his pupils dilated. "That was…"

"Very nice."

"I was going to say a lot more than that, but, yes. Very nice." He raked a hand through his shaggy hair, shaking his head slowly. A tremor of fear rippled through her.

"Simon…"

"I care about you, Anna." He turned to look at her resolutely. "I know we haven't known each other very long, and you're going back to Manchester in another week, but I care about you. I want this—us—to go somewhere." He searched her face, clearly trying to gauge her reaction. "Does that scare you off?"

"No…" Not exactly, anyway. It thrilled and terrified her

in equal measure, but was she scared off? Was she going to go rabbiting back to Manchester rather than face the possibility of a real relationship? Well, maybe. "I'm a little scared," she confessed. "Not of you. But of… this. You know I don't have a lot of experience with relationships."

"Experience can be overrated." He glanced at the clock with a sigh. "I have to get ready for the evening service now, so we'll have to continue this conversation later. Gives us some time to think, at least."

"Yes…"

"Why don't I walk you back to the vicarage?"

"Okay."

Anna waited on the sofa, replaying that lovely, lovely kiss through her mind as Simon went to get ready for the evening service. It was comfortable there, and rather novel, to be thinking about being kissed while waiting for a man to walk her home. Her mind drifted to future scenarios of seeing Simon, dating him, having a boyfriend. All quite lovely, and yet…

Where, really, could this relationship go? Was it crazy to spin it out to its conclusion before it had even begun? She was in Manchester; Simon was in Thornthwaite. Simon was going to be the *vicar* of Thornthwaite, which brought with it a whole host of challenges beyond their geography. She was so not vicar's wife material.

"Ready?" Simon came into the sitting room dressed in his black clerical shirt and dog collar, his hair brushed into dubious submission.

"Yes." Anna stood up and Simon fetched her coat; she fumbled as she tried to slip her arms in, and once again they were doing the awkward coat dance. "I'm so not good at this," she said, and, although she'd meant the coat, she realized she meant a lot of other things too. She didn't know how to do relationships, at least romantic ones. Friendship was fine, and family was a minefield, but this? Simon?

Simon rested his hands on her shoulders. "Don't overthink it, Anna," he said, and leaned his forehead against hers. "Please, not yet. Give it a chance to breathe. Give us a chance to grow."

His words both relieved and comforted her. "You really have a knack for knowing what I'm thinking."

"Maybe because I'm thinking it, too."

"Are you?" She leaned back so she could look into his eyes. "What are you thinking right now, Simon?"

"That I like you a lot and I hope you like me, but there are a fair amount of challenges to us having a relationship."

She nodded slowly, wondering what challenges he was thinking of beyond the obvious one of them living three hours apart. Was he worried about taking on another girlfriend with "issues"? Anna did not have the courage to ask him.

"Come on," he said, and he slipped his hand in hers. "Let's go."

And so she told herself not to overthink it, just as Simon

had asked her, as they stepped out into the frosty night and started walking towards the vicarage. She wouldn't give into fear, at least not yet. And, as they walked hand in hand, Anna found that was easier than she'd expected. She simply wanted to enjoy this moment for all the beauty it held.

Chapter Eleven

THE CHURCH LOOKED its most serenely beautiful for the midnight Christmas Eve carol service. Anna stepped into the soaring, candlelit space and breathed in the scent of fresh holly and evergreen, candle wax, and the usual musty church smell that felt as if it had always been a part of her.

After Simon had dropped her off at the vicarage, she'd spent a fairly fraught few hours helping her mother get ready for the wardens' tipple after the five o'clock service. She'd managed to say hello to all of them, before thankfully disappearing into the kitchen, and then they'd had their usual family Christmas Eve meal of shepherd's pie. Rachel and Dan and Will and Esther had all come, and everyone had been a bit subdued, in light of knowing this was the last such meal they'd share in the vicarage, the only family home she and her sisters had ever known.

They'd all hung their stockings afterwards, a family tradition, and Ruth had hung up Jamie's stocking, also a tradition, one that made Anna ache. It always hurt to see that empty stocking on Christmas morning, yet her mother had always been insistent it was a way to remember he was still with them, if only in memory.

Then her father had returned to church to prepare for the carol service, and Rachel and Esther had gone off; Anna had noticed that Rachel still seemed tense, and Dan looked a little unhappy. What on earth was that about?

She'd spent the rest of the evening wrapping the presents she'd bought for her family and putting them under the tree. Her mum would fill everyone's stockings; it was one of her favourite parts of Christmas, because she'd never had a stocking as a child.

"My parents were too sensible," she'd said more than once. "But I think they're just magical."

Anna was looking forward to opening all the thoughtful little treats she'd find in her stocking tomorrow morning, lovingly picked out by her mother. Ruth's thoughtful kindness never ceased to amaze and humble Anna.

At eleven-thirty, she and Ruth had headed over to church, smiling and murmuring Christmas greetings to others who were coming down the church lane. Anna had always enjoyed the special feeling of complicity and togeth-erness that the midnight service provided; everyone coming out on this cold, starry night, to share in something sacred and reverent. The church was hushed and quiet as she and Ruth sat down in a pew near the front, creamy, white candles flickering at the end of each one.

And then the service began, and Anna lost herself in the

music and majesty, the sense of expectation she always felt blossom in her on Christmas Eve.

Each carol soared upwards, voices joined together, offering both praise and thanksgiving. And she had so much to be thankful for—a family who loved her deeply, a good job, a circle of friends, Simon. Her gaze tracked him up by the altar, his expression both serious and serene. Yes, she was very thankful for Simon, even if she had no idea what, or how much, the future held.

As the service ended, people left quickly and quietly, murmuring their greetings; it was one-thirty in the morning and everyone wanted to get home. Ruth slipped out hurriedly, telling Anna she'd see her back at the vicarage; Anna knew she would be busy filling up everyone's stockings.

Anna stayed where she was as the church emptied out, savouring the stillness, trying to let her mind be peacefully blank. She hadn't realized how late it had become until she heard footsteps and then the creak of the pew as someone slid in next to her.

"Hello, Anna Banana," Roger said. "Are you all right?"

Anna looked at him, his dear, weathered face and crinkly eyes, that familiar, affable expression mixed with tender concern. The church was quiet and empty, no one there but the two of them.

"No, Dad," she whispered. "I don't think I am."

Roger's brows drew together and he put one comforting hand on his shoulder. "Darling," he said. "What is it? Will you finally tell me?"

"Finally?" she repeated in a shaky voice. "You mean, you've known…"

"Your mother and I have always been concerned for you, Anna. Staying away for so long, always so quiet. But we hoped you'd tell us if you were sad or worried about anything in your own time. Your own way."

Anna's throat was getting tighter and tighter, making it hard to speak. Harder than it usually was, which meant it was just about impossible. So she just shook her head, and then her father drew her into a big hug, her second one of the day, and just as needed.

"Anna, darling," he said. "Whatever it is, it won't change anything between us. You know that, don't you? Not one miserable little jot."

Anna squeezed her eyes shut. "D-d-d-do you think it's my fault Jamie died?"

She felt her father stiffen in surprise. "What…" he began in a distant, shocked voice, and Anna hurried to clarify.

"I know you wouldn't say you did. I kn-know you wouldn't even think it. B-b-b-but is there s-s-s-some part of you, s-s-s-some small part that does? Because I r-r-r-ran ahead and Jamie ch-chased me?"

Roger was silent for a long moment. "I have never," he finally said, each word a throb of sincerity and emotion, "thought that for one second. Not one nanosecond, not even the smallest, meanest part of me. Never, Anna? Do you understand me?" He took her by both shoulders and leaned back so he was looking at her, his expression suddenly fierce. "Never. Never. Do you believe me?"

Wordlessly, Anna nodded, because she did, and yet somehow it didn't make anything better. She still felt it. She still felt the grief, the guilt, the pain. Would it ever go away?

"Anna, oh, Anna." Her father's voice broke and he pulled her into a tight hug. "I think about him every day. I know I haven't said, but perhaps I should have. Perhaps I should have talked about him more, about that day more, to let all of you experience your grief. If I'd known you were carrying this all along… if I'd known for one minute—" He broke off and with shock Anna realized her father was crying, only the second time she'd ever seen him weep.

The first had been after Jamie's death, when he and Ruth had returned home from the hospital, after Jamie had been pronounced dead. He'd told her and her sisters the news, and then he'd broken down, his hands covering his face, his shoulders shaking.

It had been an awful moment, to see her father in thrall to such grief, and it made Anna understand why he hadn't given in to such emotion since. He'd wanted to be strong for his family, his daughters. But maybe sometimes strength didn't look or feel the way you expected it to.

"Dad, it's okay," she burst out, tears streaking down her own face, as well. "It's okay. Don't blame yourself."

He smiled at her through his tears, looking older and

wearier and more careworn than she'd ever seen him look before. "I suppose we all blame ourselves. It seemed like such a senseless tragedy, and yet I have to believe God is in that, Anna, as much as He is in any of the good things in our lives."

"I know you do." She didn't know whether she'd have the same measure of faith as her father, but she admired him for it, and the fact that he had held onto it even when his only son had died.

"Do you believe me?" he asked seriously, once they'd both managed to compose themselves and wipe the traces of tears from their faces. "That I don't blame you?"

Anna considered it, probing her tender feelings the way she would a sore tooth or an open wound. "Yes," she said at last.

"And Mum and your sisters too?"

That was a little bit harder. "I don't think they actually blame me," she said slowly, "but I've... I've always felt different." She let out a breath. "Left out."

Roger stared at her hard. "Because of Jamie's death?"

"Sort of." She'd never been this remotely honest with her father before, and it was hard now, but a good kind of hard, like the stretching of sore muscles. "Because it felt like we were meant to have this perfect family and then there was me."

Roger knit his brow. "A perfect family? Did you really think people thought of us that way?"

"Well, yes, basically." She shrugged. "You know, the family in the vicarage, everyone watching us grow up…" She couldn't count the number of times she'd had her cheek pinched or some virtual stranger recall an intimate detail of her life. But that was what growing up in the vicarage of a village meant. "And I was so…" She gulped. "Shy and quiet, I felt like I didn't fit in."

Her father's frown deepened. "I'm so sorry you felt that way, Anna. I wish I'd known. I should have known, as your father." He shook his head in regret. "I suppose I knew a bit, because of course I could see that you were shy, but I just thought that was who you were. I didn't want to push you to be someone else."

"It's not just the sh-shyness," Anna admitted in a whisper. "It's that I-I s-s-s-stammer." Her cheeks flushed. "When I'm nervous or with groups of people."

Her father stared at her for a long moment. "Anna," he said finally, "did you think I didn't know you stammered?"

Her blush deepened as realization jolted her. "But you never said anything."

"I suppose because it didn't seem important. I thought you might grow out of it, and if you didn't, then it was a part of you. A long time ago, your mother wondered if we should get you some kind of help for it, but we thought that would make you feel as if there was something wrong with you when there wasn't." Anna could only shake her head. All this time she'd held her big secret so close, and they'd *known?*

It was almost laughable, and totally surprising, and yet… some part of her recognized that it wasn't surprising at all. Of course they'd known. Her parents were loving and observant, and it wasn't something she'd been able to hide all that easily. Maybe it had simply been that she hadn't wanted them to know. That she hadn't wanted to be known.

"Should we have said something?" Roger asked seriously. "Would it have made you feel better, if we'd talked about it more?"

"Honestly? I don't know." If her parents had drawn attention to it, she might have simply retreated more. Perhaps it had taken this long to get to where she was now, able to talk, ready to heal. Hopefully.

"Anna, I feel like we failed you." Roger stared at her directly, unflinching from the stark bluntness of his statement. "You've been holding so much in, hiding it from us, and we should have been the ones to comfort and help you. We should have addressed it. If I had any idea that was what was keeping you away for so long…" He shook his head, and then touched her cheek. "I'm so sorry, my darling."

"I'm sorry, too. For-for being the way I am."

"That," Roger said firmly, "is not something you should ever be sorry for. No apology needed, ever. Your mother and I love you, have always loved you, for exactly you are. Maybe we didn't say it enough."

"You did. I knew you loved me. I knew you would always love me. It's just…" How to explain it. "I never felt good enough. And that was on me."

"No, not just on you." Roger's expression became shadowed. "The truth is, Anna, that it isn't simply a case of misunderstanding. After your brother died… your mum and I coped in different ways. I think we both shut down a little, emotionally, to all of you girls. I lost myself in work and caring for people who didn't matter so much to me. It felt easier, safer. And your mother, God bless her, did what she always does when she's worried or sad—she became very busy. But maybe in doing that we lost sight of you four, as well as of ourselves. Maybe we let some things slip that we shouldn't have, and assumed everyone was all right simply because they seemed all right on the surface. I'm sorry it's taken till now to find our way back."

"That isn't your fault," Anna said. "At least not entirely. I don't think I wanted to be found."

"And now?"

"I suppose with you and Mum moving on and everything changing, I wanted to say something. Before it's too late."

"It's never too late, Anna. That's one of the wonderful tenets of our faith. There's always time for a fresh start." He smiled at her. "But it is late now, in terms of being in this church. The heating went off at one and it's going to get very cold, very quickly. How about we head back to the vicarage for a late-night hot choc?"

A cup of tea cured her mother's ill; it was hot chocolate for her daughter. Anna smiled and sniffed. "All right, Dad."

When they stepped outside of the church, Simon was standing there, bringing them both up short.

"Simon!" Roger easily reverted to his usual affable self. "Sorry, have you been waiting?"

"Just wanted to make sure you locked up." Simon sent a questioning glance to Anna; she realized she must look a fright, with her face blotchy and red, her eyes swollen. She'd cried more today than she had in years, and yet that wasn't actually a bad thing. They were necessary tears, healing ones.

"Would you like to join us for a hot chocolate nightcap back at the vicarage?" Roger asked Simon, and he turned from Anna to smile at his boss.

"Thank you, but no. I need my beauty sleep, little good that it does me. I'll see you tomorrow morning."

"Bright and early for the nine a.m.," Roger concurred cheerfully. "Come on, darling."

Later, after a cup of hot chocolate in the cosy kitchen with her dad, Anna curled up in bed, her body and mind both exhausted. For so many years she'd been living a safe, dull life, going to work, meeting up with friends, but always keeping herself hidden and separate behind a wall of shy reserve. Today that wall had been well and truly shattered. Part of her was desperate to start reassembling it, brick by painful brick, and another part wanted to step over the rubble and walk free.

Which would she do? Which would she have the courage and conviction to do? Anna fell asleep before she could think too hard about that question, the memory of Simon's kiss the last thing that flitted through her mind before sleep thankfully overtook her.

Chapter Twelve

"HAPPY CHRISTMAS!"

Anna looked up from her morning mug of coffee to see Dan standing in the doorway, dressed in jeans and a sweater and bearing a tray of cinnamon rolls, brandishing a big smile.

"Happy Christmas," she replied, uncomfortably she was wearing fleece pyjamas, no bra, and she had a serious case of bed head, with half her hair flattened on one side and sticking up in tufts on the other. It was seven-thirty in the morning, and she hadn't expected visitors, but she supposed Dan was practically family now.

"I'll put these here," he murmured, and he set the tray on the counter. Anna took another sip of coffee, her heart sinking when Dan straightened and put his hands in his pockets as if he intended to stay awhile. She was still exhausted from being put through the emotional ringer yesterday more than once. She didn't think she could handle a heart-to-heart with Dan, especially when she had a sneaking and uncomfortable feeling that he knew, or at least suspected, she'd had a crush on him back in school.

"So, Anna," he asked as he rocked back on his heels. "How are you?" He kept her gaze in a way that made her realize he wanted a real answer, not a pat one.

"I'm okay," she said, and that was the truth. "Tired but okay."

"How do you feel about your dad's news?"

"A little sad, but happy for him too. Congratulations, by the way. I don't think I've actually said that to you since you and Rachel announced your engagement." It was funny, but just a few days ago she'd felt gutted that Rachel was dating her secret crush, but now it seemed like nearly nothing. It paled utterly in light of what she and Simon had shared, new as their relationship was.

"Thanks. It's all happened rather quickly."

"How long have you been dating, then?"

"Three months." Dan flashed her a quick, slightly abashed smile. "But when you know, you know, right?"

"Right." Did she know with Simon? It was far too early to tell, of course, and yet Anna felt a peacefulness that had settled in her bones, a peacefulness she hadn't felt in years, maybe even since before Jamie had died. She knew it was in large part to Simon, to his understanding and gentle kindness, and, yes, his kiss.

"I'm glad you've come back to Thornthwaite," Dan said, his gaze searching hers. "It seemed like you were set to stay away for a while."

"I was." Anna debated whether to say more, whether she had it in her. "As m-m-m-much as I love it here, it holds s-s-s-some hard memories." There. That hadn't been so terrible, had it?

Dan nodded slowly. "We all miss Jamie." He paused. "I remember you had a tough time at school with some mean girls."

She simply nodded, deciding to save her speech. Yes, the mean girls had been tough to deal with, and she'd been such a lamentably obvious target, a shy, socially awkward stammerer. Easy pickings. She was still shy, still stammered, but for the first time in her life she could start to see past her shortcomings and imagine the kind of future for herself that so many others took for granted. The thought was thrilling and more than a little scary.

"There you are." Rachel came into the kitchen, her hair, a shade lighter than Anna's, pulled back into a ponytail, a frown bisecting her forehead. "We're going to open the stockings before Dad heads to the first service."

"Great." Dan slid an arm around Rachel's waist and Anna didn't miss the way her sister tensed slightly before relaxing into the embrace. Something about it made Anna think her sister had had to force herself to relax. What was going on there? And if she asked Rachel, would her sister open up? As much as they all loved each other, she and her sisters hadn't actually shared the hard and intimate details of their lives.

"We should go," Rachel said, and slipped away from Dan's arm. He let out a little sigh, a flash of sadness crossing his face, and Anna followed them both into the sitting room.

The next hour was one of happy chaos, with the ripping of tissue paper and the excited shrieks of three daughters who had, for the moment at least, turned into little girls. Ruth beamed at them all, her own stocking, filled by her husband, lying forgotten and unopened. As always, their mother preferred watching others open their gifts than opening hers.

Anna was touched at the thoughtfulness her mother put into each small gift in her stocking—an intensive hand cream since she suffered from eczema; the latest cosy mystery from the series she liked to read; a new set of headphones for her commute by train to work.

"It's almost as if you're in my mind," Rachel remarked as she opened her own gifts. "How did you know I liked this shade of lipstick?"

Ruth shrugged, smiling. "It's fun, trying to think of what you'd like or what you'd need."

"You must have bought a few additions recently," Esther remarked as she held up a bottle of prenatal vitamins. "Since you didn't know I was pregnant until a few days ago."

"Yes, well." Ruth ducked her head. "I had to include the baby."

Anna sat back after she'd finished opening her stocking presents, content and yet also touched with a bittersweet sorrow. It seemed nearly impossible to believe that in a few short months the vicarage would be empty, her parents' belongings put in storage, and Ruth and Roger on the way to China. She felt a pang at the loss of connection to Thornthwaite and the vicarage; it felt a little bit like losing Jamie all over again. Did her parents feel that? Did her mother want to stay in the house where Jamie had been born, where he'd last slept? His room had been turned into a guest room years ago; there was no shrine, but there was still a remnant of connection, however fragile and ghostlike.

"I'll get a bin bag for all the tissue paper," Anna said, and headed to the kitchen, stopping short when she saw Simon there, making another pot of coffee.

"Anna." He turned to her with a glad smile, and her heart tumbled in her chest. She loved his smile. She loved his glinting eyes. She loved—

No. She couldn't think that way, didn't want to let herself fall too fast or hard. They'd known each other days. Yes, they'd bared each other's hearts and she'd kissed him in a way that she'd kissed no other man, but… days. Mere days. Plus she was still in her pyjamas, still had a severe case of bedhead.

"I didn't realize you were here." In her nervousness she sounded stiff, and Simon noticed.

"I came in while you were all opening your stockings. It seemed like a family moment, and I didn't want to intrude."

"I'm sure you would have been welcome."

"Even so." He turned back to the coffee, focusing on

spooning granules into the cafetiere. "How are you?"

"Tired. Yesterday was… emotional."

"Yes." He paused to glance at her. "You had a good conversation with your father?"

"Yes, I think so. I did as you said."

"You mean you told him—"

"Yes." Her throat was going tight in the all too familiar way and so she decided not to say anything more. Simon, bless him, merely nodded, understanding.

"I'm glad."

She nodded back, and then wordlessly he dropped the coffee scoop and pulled her into a hug. It felt like the best thing in the world, her safe haven, a place where she felt at home. *Loved.* Maybe she shouldn't be thinking that way, but with her cheek against his chest, she was.

They didn't speak as they remained in that silent embrace, needing no words. Anna wished everything in life could be this easy. This simple and straightforward, the purest form of communication, no need to stumble through syllables, just connect with truth and feeling.

Then Esther came into the kitchen and pulled herself up short. "Oh," she said.

With a slightly sheepish smile Simon gave Anna one last comforting squeeze and then stepped back. "Happy Christmas, Esther."

"Seems like it's a happy Christmas for you two," Esther returned tartly, but she smiled as she said it. Typical Esther.

"Is everyone done with the stockings?" Anna asked.

"They were done ages ago. We've been waiting for the bin bag."

"Oh, right." Anna rifled through the clutter of bottles under the sink and emerged with the required bag. "Here we are."

"I'll take it," Esther said, and held out her hand for the bag. "You two seem otherwise occupied." She left before Anna could muster a reply, not that she would have known what to say.

"I suppose we've been busted," Simon remarked as he raked a hand through his hair. It went, rather adorably, every which way when he dropped his hand. "Do you mind?"

"I don't know. It's not you, it's my family. They jump all over everything, and I'm not sure I'm ready for that. Especially…" She paused, biting her lip.

"Especially…" Simon prompted, his eyes narrowing a little.

"It's just so new—and we live in different places. Like you said last night, there are a lot of obstacles."

"Yes, there are," Simon agreed steadily. "But we don't need to tackle them all today, do we?"

"No." A wave of relief washed over her. She didn't want to tackle any of them today. She simply wanted to enjoy being with Simon… without having to think too hard about the future, or even at all.

The rest of the morning passed pleasantly; her father and

Simon headed over to the church while Anna showered and dressed and helped her mother and sisters get the Christmas dinner started. Then the men returned and they all decamped to the sitting room to open presents.

It felt remarkably relaxed and normal to have Simon among their group, along with Dan and Will. The teasing was good-natured, the conversation comfortable, and both Esther and Rachel seemed to have finally relaxed. Getting engaged or having a baby were both big things. Anna supposed it had taken her sisters some time to get used to the changes in their lives.

"Guess who I have here!" Roger announced when they'd taken a break from tearing open presents and scattering wrapping paper. He held his laptop aloft like it was a trophy. "Miriam!"

This was followed by a chorus of explanations, and then they were all crowding around the screen, peering at Miriam's remarkably clear image. She was sitting on a pristine white sand beach with the sky an azure-blue behind her.

"G'day," she greeted them in a rather bad Australian accent.

"Happy Christmas, darling," Ruth exclaimed.

"How do you have Wi-Fi on the beach?" Esther demanded.

Miriam laughed, and Anna couldn't help but notice how happy and pretty her little sister looked. Her skin was tanned and freckly, her dark hair streaked with blond from the sun and dip-dyed blue for good measure.

"I'm sitting outside the hostel where I'm staying," she explained, and moved her laptop so they could see the modest stucco building behind her.

"How are you, sweetheart?" Roger asked. "We miss having you here for Christmas."

"I know, I'm sorry not to be there." For a second Miriam looked serious. "Especially considering your news, Dad. Congratulations." Her cheeky grin returned in full force. "Perhaps I'll see you two in China."

"I certainly hope so."

"What are you up to now, anyway?" Esther asked. "For work, I mean?"

"Teaching English. It's good fun."

They continued to chat as Anna listened, amazed at the freewheeling lifestyle her sister enjoyed, without, it seemed, any plans to return home. But then this wasn't going to be home for much longer. Miriam would most likely mind the least.

After another few minutes the connection started to stall and so they all chorused goodbye, and then turned back to the last presents to open.

"This one is rather special," Ruth said, handing it to Esther. "Why don't you and Will open it together?"

Esther looked slightly suspicious but she dutifully shuffled over closer to her husband and they pulled at the paper together. Will lifted the lid of the box and after a second of simply staring at what was inside Esther lifted out a newborn sleepsuit in snowy-white velveteen, complete with a hood with pink bunny ears. Everyone oohed and aahed at the darling outfit.

"That is the sweetest thing I've ever seen," Rachel exclaimed, and Ruth beamed.

"I couldn't resist," she said to Esther. "I know it's a bit early, but I saw it when I was in town and it just looked so darling…"

"It is darling," Esther said. She folded it carefully and put it back in the box. "So sweet. Thanks, Mum."

The words were right but the tone wasn't. Although she smiled and then got up to hug her mum, Esther seemed a bit strained and wooden about it at all. Will reached for her hand when she sat back down and gave it a squeeze.

"I think we're both still a little bit in shock about the baby," he said in what Anna suspected was meant to be an apology or at least an explanation for Esther's lack of enthusiasm. "It all happened faster than we thought it would."

"Babies don't keep to a schedule," Roger said with a smile, but Anna could see her mum look at Esther with a little frown of worry. She could tell something was amiss, just as Anna could. But what on earth was it?

Later, after the presents had been opened and the wrapping paper cleared away, and her mother was checking on the roast turkey while her father stoked the fires blazing cheerily in all the downstairs rooms, Simon asked Anna if she wanted to take Charlie for a short walk before dinner.

"You can be back in time to do the Yorkshire puds," he promised, and so, feeling a heady mix of excitement and nerves, Anna pulled on her welly boots and slipped into her parka.

It was the kind of cold, clear day that stole the breath straight from her lungs. The grass glittered with frost as they crunched through it on the way to the footpath that ran the base of the fells. Although the sky was a bright blue, already, at two o'clock in the afternoon, dusky shadows were starting to lengthen.

"Do you think you'll get used to the weather up here?" Anna asked as they walked along, Charlie trotting happily at their heels. "Dark winters, light summers, and endless rain?"

"I don't mind the rain." With a smile Simon slipped his gloved hand in hers. "Makes you appreciate the sunny days even more."

"Yes, I suppose that's true." It took the bad to appreciate the good.

After feeling left out and lonely for most of her life, Anna could certainly appreciate the simple joys of this moment—Simon's hand in hers, the sun shining, Charlie trotting along next to them. If she could have stayed in this moment, she would have. Not ask for more, not settle for less.

But she couldn't stay in any moment. Life went relentlessly on whether she wanted it to or not. And even though she'd wanted simply to be, to enjoy Christmas and this time with Simon, already Anna's mind went racing ahead. She had a train ticket booked back to Manchester on December twenty-ninth. Her parents had wanted her to stay through New Year's, but she hadn't been able to get the time off work. And what would happen when she got on that train? Would they make a long-distance relationship work, and for how long?

Simon needed to be in Thornthwaite. As for her… could she come back here? There was no job, for one, and even though she knew it was silly and even dangerous to think this way, this much, she couldn't see herself as a vicar's wife. Teaching Sunday school, hosting everything, always in the village's public eye. All of it terrified her, plus she knew she wouldn't be good at it. So what then?

"Anna," Simon said, and he squeezed her hand. "Whatever you're thinking about, stop."

"What do you mean?"

He tugged on her hand so she had to turn to face him, and they stopped, Charlie sprawling across their boots. Gently, Simon touched her forehead with his gloved thumb. "You get a little furrow there when you're worried."

"You know that about me already?"

"I know a lot of things about you already."

"That's true." Her smile wobbled, his thumb still brushing her forehead.

Then he slid his hand down to cup her cheek, the glove rough against her skin, and then he leaned forward and she did too, and then they were kissing. Feeling his mouth move on hers again felt like such a *relief.* She hadn't realized she'd been waiting for this, just this, since the last time he'd kissed her yesterday. Their hips and noses both bumped as they continued to kiss, lovely feelings of heat and need swirling through her, until Charlie whined and with a little laugh Simon stepped back.

"Sorry, I was getting a bit carried away there."

"I didn't mind." Anna couldn't keep herself from blushing. "But I don't suppose you want all of Thornthwaite gossiping about you before you've barely begun your curacy."

"I don't care about gossip." Simon looked at her seriously. "Anna… my position here… does it put you off at all? From thinking about us?"

His gaze was so direct, the question so honest, that for a moment she couldn't answer. Her family was wonderful in their own way, but they weren't honest about things like this. They didn't ask the hard questions and then wait for the answers, wanting to know. Not like Simon did.

"A bit," she felt compelled to admit. "I'm not…" She could not tell him she didn't think she was vicar's wife material. Mentioning the word "wife" when they were barely dating was an extreme no-no. "There's a lot to consider, I suppose."

"Yes, there always is." Simon was still looking at her seriously, peering at her as if trying to divine some mystery from her expression. "I really hope it doesn't put you off," he said at last.

Anna couldn't keep a grin from spreading across her face at his heartfelt tone. "Thank you," she said, and then dared to lean forward and kiss him again.

She'd meant simply to brush his lips but he grabbed her arm and pulled her closer, and a sizzle of both longing and excitement blazed through her at the hunger she felt in his touch. For her. It felt like a gift, a miracle.

Eventually they broke apart and started walking back towards the vicarage. The light had been leached from the sky, leaving it bone-white with shadows gathering on the horizon, the fells already cloaked in twilit darkness.

Simon took her hand and Anna smiled at him in the dark, for once in her life feeling happy despite the fear, with the fear. She might never conquer her innate shyness and social anxiety, but she could savour this moment… and more moments like this, when they came.

Back at the vicarage, Roger called Simon into his study to discuss some change to Sunday's service, and Anna headed back to the kitchen to do the Yorkshire puddings. She stopped in the doorway, shocked to see Esther sitting at the kitchen table, her head buried in her arms.

"Esther…"

Esther looked up, red-eyed and sniffly. "I'm fine," she said in a clogged voice, but with a flash of warning in her eyes. Of all the Holley sisters, Esther liked scenes the least, and Anna suspected her oldest sister equated emotion with weakness.

"Okay," she said cautiously, unsure where to go with the conversation. Esther was so clearly not all right. Anna reached for a bowl and measuring jug and began to mix the Yorkshire pudding batter. "Do you want to talk about it?" she asked eventually. Esther was simply sitting at the table, staring into space.

"Not really," she answered on a sigh. "Not at all, because you'll think I'm either mad or an ungrateful cow, and I'm probably both."

"Try me," Anna said. "Maybe I won't think you're either."

Esther took a shuddering breath, her gaze downcast. "Oh, Anna," she said, and she sounded so sad, so broken, that Anna nearly wept. "The truth is… the terrible truth is… I don't want this baby."

Chapter Thirteen

SIMON GAZED AT Anna from across their table at The Queen's Sorrow and could only think how fast it had all gone. Just three days since Christmas, and he'd spent them all with Anna. On Boxing Day, they'd driven to St. Bees on the coast, and watched as all the local farmers had driven their tractors onto the wide, flat stretch of damp sand. Children had run to and fro, scrambling on top of the mechanical beasts, while the farmers had looked on, either stony-faced or smiling.

Afterwards they'd walked up to the Head, battling brisk winds and an alarmingly steep climb but the view of the sea stretching on endlessly, the Isle of Man a violet smudge on the horizon, had been worth it.

On the way back to Thornthwaite, they'd stopped at a cosy pub tucked up in the fells for lunch and it had all felt so perfect, the conversation easy and comfortable, the kisses stolen in private moments heart-stoppingly wonderful, the future shining ahead of them like a golden promise.

Yesterday, they'd spent with Anna's family, tidying up

after Christmas and taking a walk through the village. Simon had started to sense some of the cracks and currents running through all the Holleys—Rachel's engagement, Esther's pregnancy, Roger's retirement. A lot was changing, and change, whether good or bad, was also hard. Today he'd had to work in the morning—he did have a job, after all—but in the afternoon he and Anna drove to Buttermere and walked around the lake. It had been lovely, the rolling fells a perfect backdrop to the nestled jewel of the lake, but it had also been freezing and halfway through a needling, icy sleet had started to fall, leaving them both cold and wet and miserable, hurrying to make it all the way around.

They'd warmed up in a pub but already Simon had had that awful, sinking suspicion that Anna was slipping away, going too quiet, not meeting his eye, and he'd been amazed at how familiar that felt. How awful.

It had been the same with Ellie. She'd stopped taking her medication without telling him and, at first, he'd told himself he'd been imagining things. The silence wasn't sullen; she was just quiet. They weren't talking because they were busy. Everything was fine. But it hadn't been, and if he'd seen it earlier, maybe, just maybe, he could have done something.

Simon knew thinking that way was pointless torture, but with Anna going quiet on him he couldn't help it. He went there in his mind, in his heart. Instantly. It was impossible not to. He'd soldiered on and now it was Anna's last night and they were having dinner in The Queen's Sorrow. Tomorrow she was taking the train back to Manchester, and they hadn't yet discussed when or if they'd see each other again.

"It all went rather quickly in the end, didn't it?" Simon remarked as they perused menus.

Anna had been reluctant to come to the pub because she felt she'd know too many people, something which Simon had tried not to let irritate or, worse, hurt him because they were a couple, weren't they? Right now that seemed somewhat uncertain.

"Mmm." Anna kept her gaze on the menu and Simon stared at her helplessly, wishing he wasn't facing this quiet yet determined emotional retreat. He hated how it made him doubt. Perhaps he wasn't capable of handling the highs and lows of any relationship. Perhaps he wasn't strong enough.

"Anna."

She looked up, her expression turning wary as she saw how serious he looked. But she was leaving *tomorrow.* They couldn't skate past that reality any longer.

"Talk to me. When will I see you again?" He sounded needy and urgent, something else he hated. Ellie had hated it too. *Just give me some space, Si,* she'd snarl at him, and he'd blink at her, so startled by the sudden viciousness. Then he'd tiptoe away and give her the space she said she needed, a choice he still wasn't sure had been the right one. It was a choice he didn't want to make now.

"I… I don't know." His heavy heart sank even further.

"You don't?"

"You work on weekends and I work weekdays. It makes it difficult, doesn't it?"

"Yes." Another one of those obstacles he'd talked about in such vague terms. When he'd first met Anna, he'd felt like a superhero, tossing obstacles and objections out of the way as if they were nothing, so sure that together they could make this work. But now he wondered whether they could, and he knew Anna was wondering too. He wasn't a superhero. He wasn't even strong. Being in a relationship again, however tentative or tenuous, made him realize that afresh.

Anna didn't answer and Simon made himself ask, "How difficult does it make it, Anna?"

She tensed and he wished he hadn't gone there, laid it out so plainly. He'd given her an out, and he had a horrible feeling she was going to take it.

"I don't know, Simon." Anna lowered her gaze and he fought a wave of frustration. "Everything's still so new… and so much is changing…"

"There you are!"

Now they were both tensing as Simon turned to smile at a woman he recognized from church but whose name he didn't yet know. She obviously knew them, because she was gazing at them with benevolent if beady interest.

"How nice that you're having dinner together," she said, and cocked her head. "Have you two known each other long?"

"A little while," Simon said pleasantly. "Have you had a nice Christmas?"

"Oh, lovely, lovely, as always. The carol service is always such a wonderful service." The woman, with her comfortable bosom and florid, farmer's wife face, turned to Anna.

"How are you, my dear? Still holed up in Manchester?"

Anna's smile froze on her face. She answered carefully, "Yes. I live there."

"You do seem to have kept away from us, lovey," the woman chided. "Why is that?"

Anna swallowed and then said, "N-n-n-no reason." A blush swept over her face and she looked away.

"It's so nice to see you," Simon intervened. "I hope you have a lovely meal."

The woman looked slightly taken aback and Simon had a bad feeling he'd offended her. He also found he didn't much care. Maybe this was why Anna hadn't wanted to go to The Queen's Sorrow.

The woman left with both a smile and a huff, and when she'd gone Anna shook her head. "You can't make enemies like that, Simon. Not when you're going to be vicar."

"*That* was making an enemy?"

"That's village life," she replied with a shrug. "People want a part of you all the time." She looked away, and he saw sadness clinging to her features like cobwebs. Felt it in himself.

"Anna…"

"Why don't we order?"

⟫⟫⟫⟪⟪⟪

THIS WASN'T GOING to work. That was the staccato drumbeat of fear pulsing through her veins as they ordered their food and attempted to reassemble the pleasant and comfortable atmosphere they'd been enjoying for the last few days, but the more they tried to hold onto it the more it slipped away. Why did everything have to fall apart so soon and so fast? Yet had she really expected it not to?

The last few days had been wonderful in their own way. Walks and kisses and sweet, sweet time together. Of course, there had been some stresses. After Esther had blurted out that she didn't want the baby, she'd clammed up and Anna hadn't been able to get another word out of her. Rachel seemed tense too, and both her sisters' unhappiness had leached into their time together as a family. But Anna's time with Simon had felt separate and special… and now it seemed as if it was coming to an end.

Misery churned inside her as their food came and even Simon stopped trying to keep up the chat. It was as if they knew it was already over.

"Who was that harridan, as a matter of interest?" he finally asked as she stared down at her fish and chips and tried to summon an appetite.

"Diana Tomlinson. She's a member of the choir."

"Ah."

"You really shouldn't have dismissed her like that, Simon. Not for my sake."

"It was just as much for mine. We're having dinner."

"I know, but…"

"Even in a place like Thornthwaite, there have to be boundaries."

Her father had said the same thing, but he'd been so genial about everything no one ever felt brushed off. And she saw, in a moment of painful, piercing clarity, how their relationship wasn't going to work, not just because of her, but because of Simon. How they were together. He was always going to feel like he had to cover or compensate for her, and she would feel even more like a failure. A screw-up.

"Simon," she burst out, and he narrowed his eyes.

"Don't say it."

"You know it's true."

"Do I?"

Even though it felt like she had to rip the words from her chest, leaving gaping wounds, she made herself say them. "It's not going to work between us." Tears filled her eyes and she blinked them back, refusing to give in to her sadness. "You see it too, I think. You've been seeing it all week."

"No, I haven't." There was a stubborn set to Simon's jaw that she hadn't seen before. "What I have been seeing," he continued in a hard voice she hadn't heard before, "is you trying to keep your distance. Staying safe, perhaps."

It was a fair comment, because part of her had been inching into retreat mode as a matter of habit. When things got intense, she went into hiding. "Only because I realized more and more this can't go anywhere."

"Can't?" Simon challenged. "Or won't?"

"Maybe both," Anna admitted. "I'm not right for you, Simon."

"Maybe you're not," Simon agreed, "but you're not even giving me a chance to find out."

"Because it's too hard," she exclaimed, and then quickly lowered her voice. The last thing she wanted a scene in The Queen's Sorrow. "I don't want to start caring about you only to have my heart broken into pieces. I doubt you want that, either."

"Of course I don't. But it doesn't mean that I'm not willing to take the risk." He stared at her, seeming almost angry, and she stared back, feeling hopeless.

"I d-d-d-don't want to get hurt," she said quietly. "M-m-m-maybe that makes me a coward. But it's the truth."

"Then you're going to live a very lonely, boring life," Simon said. "Because everything good in life involves taking a risk. Being willing to get hurt."

Ouch. Maybe she'd expected a little more sympathy from him, but she wasn't seeing it in his face. And it made her realize even more how wrong they were for each other. Maybe Simon didn't have the patience for her worries and nerves, because he'd dealt with it all before. Ellie had dragged her feet and kept pulling back; maybe Simon knew this time he wanted something different. And Anna didn't know how to be different. She'd hardly ever taken a risk in her life.

They ate the rest of their meal in dismal silence, and then he walked her back to the vicarage. The sky was black and starless, the air frigid and damp. They stood outside the weathered sandstone steps of the vicarage and blinked at each other in the darkness.

"So, is this it?" Simon asked, a wobble in his voice, and Anna felt she had no choice but to nod.

"I guess it is."

He held out his hand for her to shake, which only hurt her more. All those lovely kisses… "Goodbye, Anna."

She could barely squeeze the words out of her throat. "Goodbye, Simon."

They shook hands and then, afraid she was about to burst into tears, Anna turned and walked into the vicarage.

The house was quiet even though it was only a little after nine. Her parents were probably upstairs in the TV room, watching whatever latest BBC drama had caught their fancy. Rachel was back at her house, and Esther and Will were at theirs. Walking slowly up the steps, Anna felt lonelier than she had in a long time.

She paused at the top of the stairs; the door to the TV room was partially ajar and she knew she could walk in there and see her parents curled up on the sofa in front of the fire, the telly on. They'd welcome her in and pass her popcorn and fill her in on whatever program she'd missed. She wasn't really alone, not the way she'd felt for so long. She knew that now, and yet…

She didn't want her family right now, the love and acceptance from them that she'd always had even if she hadn't felt it. It was important, essential, and yet right now she wanted Simon.

Slowly, Anna walked down the wide upstairs hall with its high ceiling and diamond-paned window at the end, overlooking the rest of the village. How many games had they played in the hall, using it as a bowling alley or a dodgeball court? She could almost hear Jamie's laughter echoing in the high-ceilinged space as he challenged his sisters to play with him.

She still missed him. She would always miss him. That wouldn't change, but maybe she could fight it less. Accept it more. Grief was a part of her. And now she had a new grief, fresh and raw, from losing Simon. From pushing him away. Yet what else could she have done?

Anna walked to the door in the middle of hallway, the second smallest bedroom sandwiched between two larger ones. One of the bigger bedrooms had been made into the TV room and one had been Esther and Rachel's. This bedroom remained unused, the door closed.

Now she opened it, holding her breath. Of course the room looked completely different. Long ago, Ruth and

Roger had decided to pack up Jamie's things and turn the little room into a guest bedroom. It remained one, with a double bed with a plaid duvet, an empty bureau, and a chair stuck in the corner. Devoid of personality, of memories, except she still felt the lingering remnant of Jamie's presence. Once the room had been messy, the bedclothes rumpled, the floor covered in bits of Lego. She could picture it now, even though it had been decades since it had looked like that. Since Jamie had been alive.

Letting out a long, low breath, Anna sat gingerly on the bed. The room was freezing, with the door closed against the heat of the rest of the house. She saw frost on the inside of the window pane.

Had she made a mistake? The question echoed emptily through her. Had she acted out of fear and self-protection as she always did, and pushed Simon away for no purpose? And yet he'd gone. He hadn't put up much of a fight in the end. That hurt, even though Anna knew it was unreasonable. What had she expected? For Simon to never take no for an answer?

Well, maybe. A little. And maybe that was part of the problem. She'd wanted him to do all the heavy lifting. She hadn't met him halfway in anything. Looking back, she could see that it wasn't fair. And yet she didn't know how she could have acted otherwise. She was still the person she was, and Simon was—

A sudden, loud hammering came from downstairs.

Someone was knocking on the front door. Violently. Anna froze as she heard her father come out of the TV room.

"Do you think someone's ill, Roger?" Ruth called worriedly. "Or worse?"

"It sounds urgent," her father called back.

He sounded just as worried as his wife. People didn't knock on the vicarage door late at night like that unless something was wrong. Anna tiptoed to the door of Jamie's old bedroom and strained to listen. She heard the creak of the front door opening, and Charlie's lethargic lumbering down the stairs to sniff the newcomer out.

And then her father's surprised exclamation—"Simon!"

Simon. Anna slipped out of the room to the top of the stairs.

"Sorry to disturb you, Roger," Simon said, sounding unaccountably grim, "but I need to speak to Anna."

"Anna?" Roger sounded surprised. "But I thought she was with you."

"No, she came back. Haven't you seen here?"

"I'm here," Anna called softly, and then she started walking down the stairs. Her heart was pounding, although with fear or excitement she couldn't say. Both, no doubt. She turned the corner in the stairs and nearly stumbled at the fierce look in Simon's eyes as he caught sight of her.

"Anna, I handled everything wrong," he said, and Roger's look of affable bemusement turned to one of genuine bafflement. Anna almost laughed.

"I was just thinking the same thing, about me," she said in little more than a whisper. It was hard to speak up but at least she wasn't stammering. Not this time.

"You were?" Relief flashed across his dear features. "I shouldn't have let you go—"

"And I don't think I should be here," Roger murmured. "I still want to catch the end of *Doctor Foster*." He hurried upstairs, shooting Ana a quick, encouraging grin as he passed her.

"I'm sorry," Simon said. "I shouldn't have said what I did."

"What exactly are you apologizing for?"

He shook his head, impatient with himself. "I was hurt and a little angry that you were willing to give up on us before we'd barely begun. But I gave up too. And I did that before, Anna. I backed off because I thought it was the right thing to do, but it's just another form of fear." He took a step towards her and reached for her hand. His long, lean fingers twined with hers. "You're scared. I understand that. I feel it, too. It's hard, so hard, to let someone in, especially when you might lose them."

"It's not just that," Anna whispered. Simon's honesty compelled her to offer him her own. "Simon, the truth is… the truth is… I'd make an awful vicar's wife." He stared at her silently for a few seconds and a flush began to spread across her face. "I know I'm rushing ahead here and jumping the gun on a million things, but I can't help but think it.

Feel it. I'm all wrong for you. I can't teach Sunday school, or lead anything or speak from the front…"

"I'm not looking for a vicar's wife, Anna," Simon said as he drew her gently towards him. "I'm not interviewing for a job position. I'm not accepting applications here."

"I know, but—"

"Sshh. For a second, please." He drew her even closer to him so that they nearly bumped noses. "I don't care about any of that. I know some people might, but they don't have anything to do with you and me."

"Still," she protested, "I don't want to feel like I'm letting you down. Like…" It hurt to say it, but she did. "Like I'm too broken for you."

Simon froze, his stare seeming to bore right into her. "Too broken for me?" he repeated. "Do you really think that?"

"Sort of," she whispered.

"I'm just as broken as you. I genuinely believe everyone's broken in one way or another, but since we're talking about us I'll keep to the point." His smile was both wry and sad. "Do you think I just bounced back from Ellie's death? It broke me into pieces. And part of me will always be in pieces, just as you will be, from your own grief. I don't want someone who isn't broken, Anna, because it's only when we've been broken that we can truly know what it means to be healed and whole. And together, maybe, we can both be that. Please, please don't ever think you're too broken, or you've got too many issues, or you aren't good enough." Suddenly he sounded fierce. "Because if that's the case, then I'm not good enough for you."

"Maybe," she suggested, her smile wobbling all over her face, "then we should both be not-good-enough for each other."

"Maybe," Simon agreed. He brushed the whisper of a kiss across her lips. "I like the sound of that."

Anna stepped into the comforting shelter of his arms and closed her eyes. She had no idea what was going to happen, or how they were going to make it work, but she realized those things didn't matter quite as much as she'd thought they did. Taking this step towards Simon, towards life and love, was the most important one. And Simon had taken that step as well, and together they would walk hand in hand into the future… and whatever it held.

The End

Read the second Holley Sister story,
about Esther and Will,
out in January 2018

The Holley Sisters of Thornthwaite series

Welcome to Thornwaite, a quaint village tucked up in England's beautiful but rainy Lake District… where homecomings happen and surprises are in store for the four Holley sisters…

Book 1: *A Vicarage Christmas*

Book 2: Coming Soon

Book 3: Coming Soon

Book 4: Coming Soon

Available now at your favorite online retailer!

About the Author

After spending three years as a diehard New Yorker, **Kate Hewitt** now lives in the Lake District in England with her husband, their five children, and a Golden Retriever. She enjoys such novel things as long country walks and chatting with people in the street, and her children love the freedom of village life—although she often has to ring four or five people to figure out where they've gone off to.

She writes women's fiction as well as contemporary romance under the name Kate Hewitt, and whatever the genre she enjoys delivering a compelling and intensely emotional story.

You can find out more about Katharine on her website at kate-hewitt.com.

Thank you for reading

A Vicarage Christmas

If you enjoyed this book, you can find more from all our great authors at TulePublishing.com, or from your favorite online retailer.

Printed in Great Britain
by Amazon